"I Have Made A Promise To You," Sakir Whispered.

"I know," Rita said breathlessly. "I'm not afraid of this happening."

On a growl, Sakir rolled, was poised atop her in seconds. "It is the need for you that I fear. There is such desperation running through my blood."

"What are you desperate for?" she asked him.

"I have wanted you since the day we met. I want you now."

Rita couldn't believe what she was hearing. Her illusive fantasy was admitting that he wanted her.

Was it the magic of the desert that had spurred this on?

She pressed her hips up. "Take me, then."

"And tomorrow?" he asked, his gaze steady but passion filled.

"I won't question tomorrow. We'll leave whatever happens between us right here."

Sakir didn't move for a moment, then he lowered his face to hers. "It is impossible."

She wasn't sure what he was referring to. She didn't know, didn't care. "Impossible, probably. But inescapable, I think."

Dear Reader,

Welcome to another fabulous month at Silhouette Desire, where we offer you the best in passionate, powerful and provocative love stories. You'll want to delve right in to our latest DYNASTIES: THE DANFORTHS title with Anne Marie Winston's highly dramatic *The Enemy's Daughter*—you'll never guess who the latest Danforth bachelor has gotten involved with! And the steam continues to rise when Annette Broadrick returns to the Desire line with a brand-new series, THE CRENSHAWS OF TEXAS. These four handsome brothers will leave you breathless, right from the first title, *Branded*.

Read a Silhouette Desire novel from *his* point of view in our new promotion MANTALK. Eileen Wilks continues this series with her highly innovative and intensely emotional story *Meeting at Midnight*. Kristi Gold continues her series THE ROYAL WAGER with another confirmed bachelor about to meet his match in *Unmasking the Maverick Prince*. How comfortable can *A Bed of Sand* be? Well, honey, if you're lying on it with the hero of Laura Wright's latest novel…who cares! And the always enjoyable Roxanne St. Claire, whom *Publishers Weekly* calls "an author who's on the fast track to making her name a household one," is scorching up the pages with *The Fire Still Burns*.

Happy reading,

Melissa Jeglinski

Melissa Jeglinski
Senior Editor, Silhouette Desire

Please address questions and book requests to:
Silhouette Reader Service
U.S.: 3010 Walden Ave., P.O. Box 1325, Buffalo, NY 14269
Canadian: P.O. Box 609, Fort Erie, Ont. L2A 5X3

A Bed of Sand

LAURA WRIGHT

Silhouette® Desire

Published by Silhouette Books

America's Publisher of Contemporary Romance

SILHOUETTE BOOKS

ISBN 0-373-76607-6

A BED OF SAND

Copyright © 2004 by Laura Wright

Visit Silhouette Books at www.eHarlequin.com

Printed in U.S.A.

Books by Laura Wright

Silhouette Desire

Cinderella & the Playboy #1451
Hearts Are Wild #1469
Baby & the Beast #1482
Charming the Prince #1492
Sleeping with Beauty #1510
Ruling Passions #1536
Locked Up with a Lawman #1553
Redwolf's Woman #1582
A Bed of Sand #1607

LAURA WRIGHT

has spent most of her life immersed in the world of acting, singing and competitive ballroom dancing. But when she started writing romance, she knew she'd found the true desire of her heart! Although born and raised in Minneapolis, Laura has also lived in New York City, Milwaukee and Columbus, Ohio. Currently she is happy to have set down her bags and made Los Angeles her home. And a blissful home it is—one that she shares with her theatrical production manager husband, Daniel, and three spoiled dogs. During those few hours of downtime from her beloved writing, Laura enjoys going to art galleries and movies, cooking for her hubby, walking in the woods, lazing around lakes, puttering in the kitchen and frolicking with her animals. Laura would love to hear from you. You can write to her at P.O. Box 5811, Sherman Oaks, CA 91413 or e-mail her at laurawright@laurawright.com.

To all my fellow romance readers
who love a tall, dark and sexy sheikh…

Prologue

There is a place in the northern desert of Joona where a man can race his stallion straight into the coming sunset. A place where amber veins run through pale sand like a thousand snakes beneath your feet, and white rocks rise straight up into a seamless blue sky. A place where the air is scented with heat and spicy wild brush, and the gods—the watchers of this land—stand erect in their sacred pools and welcome all those who risk so much in coming here.

This place is Emand.

An ancient land, rich with oil, beautiful valleys and vast cultures. But a land great with sorrow and bitter hearts.

This land bore three sons before claiming their fa-

ther. Though broken in spirit, the eldest son understood his position and remained in his homeland to rule. The younger son, destined to follow his great father, surrendered to the gods at just fifteen years of age. And the second son, Sheikh Sakir Ibn Yousef Al-Nayhal, left his home in search of his soul. But what he found instead were the strange deserts of Texas and the emptiness of a man who belonged nowhere and to no one.

One

"**W**hat a waste," Rita Thompson muttered, taking one last look at herself in the full-length mirror.

It was all there. Everything to be admired in a late-summer bride. Killer white dress—strapless, of course—white satin sandals to give her a little height, tulle veil to cover her anxious expression and a classy French manicure on both fingers and toes.

Fabulous.

And she hadn't forgotten those simple traditions of a bride-to-be either. She'd assigned her eyes as the sacred "something blue" and her sister's pearl earrings as the "something borrowed." But when it came to the "something new," she'd decided to pass.

Hey, she'd foot the bill for this entire ceremony and

the "I'm-really-sorry-about-deceiving-all-of you" reception afterward. She wasn't about to pay for anything else. Especially for herself.

She grimaced at her wedding-white reflection. "Maybe someday, kid. If you're lucky."

"If who's lucky?"

Rita turned, saw her dad in the doorway of the Paradise Lake Lodge, looking very dapper in his dove-gray suit and matching boots. "Me. I'm lucky. Got a great family and I'm not too shy to say it."

"Rita, darlin'," he said, walking toward her, "you've never been too shy for anything."

A deep pang of guilt invaded Rita's heart as her father stood before her, his eyes so kind and loving. She'd never lied to him before. Sure, she'd omitted certain things as a rowdy teenager, but this situation was entirely different.

She'd directly deceived him.

A cold knot formed in her stomach. Hopefully he'd understand why she'd gone to all the trouble of faking her engagement and marriage, and forgive her.

"You look very handsome, Dad."

"Thank you. Thank you." Ben Thompson grinned and poked out his elbow in her direction. "Ready to be escorted down the aisle, beautiful lady?"

Though a little forced, she returned his smile and slipped her arm through his. "As I'll ever be."

Her father squeezed her to him, then a sudden seriousness crept into his tone. "You're sure about this, right?"

She swallowed hard. "Of course."

He shrugged, said, "Alrighty," then led her down the Lodge steps and out into the glorious sunshine and easy lake breeze.

"You know," he continued, obviously undeterred by her assurances of premarital happiness. "I tried to have a little talk with your intended, but he hadn't arrived as yet. Cutting it pretty close, isn't he?"

"He's a very busy man."

"Maybe so, but I don't like it." He led her toward the lakeside where fifty or so guests sat in white chairs facing a lacy canopy. "Not the best way to start off with a new family."

"Don't worry. He's wonderful, Dad—and he'll be here." Interesting, she mused. She sounded completely convincing. Just the way a woman ready to take the plunge with the man of her dreams would sound.

Well, the *dreams* part was actually pretty accurate. She'd had a serious crush on her boss, Sheikh Sakir Al-Nayhal, for close to three years now. He was intelligent, intense and over-the-top sexy.

Her type in a nutshell.

But alas, the man didn't even know she was alive— below the neck, at any rate.

Rita was the best at what she did, an assistant to die for, and Sakir treated her as such, with the utmost respect. But he never looked at her as anything more than a highly competent business associate. At least, he'd never shown any signs of interest. No requests to stay late for work—unless, of course, it really *was* for work.

No lengthy glances at her legs or a knowing smile when she'd worn something just a little bit revealing to work, hoping he'd notice.

Of course, that lack of interest—though thoroughly depressing for her as a woman—was exactly why she'd chosen him as her mock fiancé. Well, that and the fact that he rarely came to Paradise and was just this minute having a business lunch with Harvey Arnold in Boston—a lunch she'd set up two months ago.

"I still can't believe we haven't met him." Her father sighed as they reached the little staging area several yards from the altar. "It's not right."

"Save your breath, Dad." Ava, Rita's older sister, sidled up to them, looking like a goddess in her pale pink satin bridesmaid dress. "Rita knows what she's doing."

"Listen to my matron of honor, Dad."

"*Maid* of honor," Ava corrected her with a smile. "For three more weeks, anyway."

Rita glanced past her sister to a gorgeous Cheyenne man sitting near the altar. His grandmother, Muna, was on his right and his newly found daughter sat perched like a happy little bird on his lap. Rita smiled, felt a deep sense of peace. She'd really done it. This little bit of deceit had been worth everything. Ava was back with the man she loved, their daughter finally had a father and a loving family, and the marriage that should've, but never had, happened four years ago was now just weeks away.

Rita gave her father's arm a squeeze. "Let's get this party started."

"Just waiting on the groom, daughter."

Rita mentally rolled her eyes. "He'll be coming out with the preacher."

Or not.

Her father led her to within feet of the white carpet stretched out over the grass, the carpet that led straight to the altar. Several of the guests turned and saw her, then quickly dropped into a low hush. Beside her, the string quartet sat at attention, ready to play.

Rita took a deep breath, released it, and clenched her fists around her sweaty palms. All she wanted to do was get this over with, get jilted and get going, off to New Orleans for beignets and Hurricanes.

"There's Reverend Chapman," Ava whispered from beside her.

"Where?" their father asked.

"Right there, Dad. He's—" Ava stopped short.

"Holy hell," Ben said, his eyes narrowed.

Nerves punched in Rita's blood.

"He's alone," Ben whispered. "What the devil is going on—"

"Dad, please." Ava touched her sister's shoulder, squeezed.

Rita lifted her chin. She was ready to hear the cheerless whispers of her friends and family as they realized her fiancé wasn't coming. She was ready to blush and force a few tears.

She was ready to flee in shame.

Then suddenly her gaze caught on a decidedly male figure, proud as a prince and dressed in a white caftan striding across the grass toward the lonely Reverend Chapman.

Rita's heart jolted, and she felt as weak as one of the reeds blowing against the lake's surface.

This wasn't possible. Not possible.

But then again, there he was.

Her boss, her fictional fiancé and her bone-melting crush, Sakir Al-Nayhal had arrived.

Uninvited and totally unabashed.

With her heart fluttering somewhere between her chest and her white satin sandals, Rita watched him walk, stared as he came to stand at the altar, tall, broad and desperately gorgeous, his dark skin eating up the paleness of his caftan.

Then he turned and looked down the aisle, looked straight at Rita, his dark green eyes and firm, sensual mouth humorless.

Rita swallowed hard as her mind raced and the world spun.

Sakir arched an eyebrow, thrust out a hand toward her as if commanding her to come to him.

"Wow," Ava said beside her. "I hadn't expected him to be so…"

Panic welling in her throat, Rita cursed under her breath and muttered, "And I hadn't expected him—period."

Two

Sakir studied her closely, wondering if she would turn around and run from him and from this place.

But escape was not in this woman's nature, he believed. Rita Thompson was the only woman he knew who walked straight into conflict and faced it head-on. She relished the opportunity to fight for what she wanted and continually asked to be challenged. These were the primary reasons he had hired her to begin with, and why he had insisted she work with him on all projects.

But he was not looking for conflict from the beautiful woman before him—not today.

He was here on a matter of business.

He needed Rita Thompson to marry him, and although this wedding day had started as a charade, he would go to any lengths to make certain it ended in a legal union.

The quartet to Rita's right began a soft, simple rendition of *The Wedding March*. The light sound filled the air around them all, causing the crowd to hush and rise to its feet.

Rita continued to stare at him, confusion and panic flashing in her spectacular blue eyes. Then, just as he wondered if perhaps she might surprise him and turn and leave, she blew out a breath, picked up the skirt of her gown and walked toward him.

Sakir watched her hips sway with the movement, watched her breasts—full and pale under the bright sun—rise and fall.

Why must the woman look so beautiful?

Over the last few years, he had rarely allowed himself the pleasure of watching Rita Thompson. She was his employee. And very valuable to him, in that respect. He would do nothing to risk losing her.

But there *were* times, at night, in his bed when he thought of this woman in ways and in positions he knew he should not. There were times when he could not help but wonder how her mouth would taste, how her sweet curves would feel beneath him, how she would turn wild in his arms as he raked his hands up her back, up her neck until his fingers threaded deep into her long tawny hair.

Sakir felt need in his groin and a surge of possessiveness in his gut, but thrust both aside. This was how he always felt when he was near her—just as he always forced himself to respond with cool indifference.

Rita was his assistant, the one woman he trusted and relied upon above all others. No matter how strong his desire for her, he knew he must suppress it in order to keep her, for a woman rebuffed—as she would most

surely be in time—would certainly leave his employ
straightaway.

Sakir stood tall as she approached him with an un-
easy expression. The music gracefully fell away and he
reached for her hand. But, as he expected, Rita was not
to be appeased. She raised a severe brow at him and kept
her arms stiffly at her sides.

Her chin set, she turned to Reverend Chapman. "I
need to speak to my…fiancé for a minute."

"Now?" the man asked, his mouth creased into a frown.

Rita nodded, said firmly, "Now." She then faced
Sakir and through gritted teeth, whispered, "Can we
talk, please?"

This was the woman he knew. Sakir suppressed a
grin. Rita Thompson would not enter into anything
without a discussion, and it pleased him to know that
even in matters such as these she was a cool thinker.

He nodded. "Of course." And again, offered her his
hand.

But she looked at his hand as if it were a venomous
spider and didn't touch him. She turned to her father,
sister and the crowd and said calmly, "If you will excuse us for a moment."

Clearly, the guests were stunned, and no doubt intrigued, by this strange turn of events, but Sakir saw that
Rita was too preoccupied to notice. She was gone from
his side in a flash, hurrying down to the water's edge.
She was already pacing back and forth by the time Sakir
joined her.

But when he did, she whirled on him and flipped her
veil over her head. "What the hell do you think you're
doing?"

His voice remained low, calm. "Should I not be asking you the very same question?"

She avoided this. "You're supposed to be in Boston."

"When I had heard I was to marry, I returned home at once."

Her gaze flickered to the grassy wetness beneath her feet, her teeth tugged at her lower lip.

He shrugged. "I thought it appropriate to attend my own wedding ceremony."

Again, she whizzed past the central question of the morning. "So, who squealed on me? Sasha? No, I'll bet it was Greg. He was always a butt-kisser."

"This does not matter, Rita."

"It does to me—"

"It is a policy of mine to know what my employees are doing. At all times. Especially when *I* am involved in what they are doing."

She narrowed her eyes, stepped closer to him. "Are you spying on me, Sakir?"

The sweet, honey scent of her stroked his senses and he felt the urge to take her in his arms and make love to her mouth. But he would not. "No, I am not spying on you. But it seems I would have good reason in doing so."

She looked away.

"What is this all about, Rita?"

Rita felt completely deflated and just wanted to lie down in the grass and cry. Her flawless plan had just exploded in her face. And the man before her, this gorgeous man with native dress and a knee-buckling gaze, was the one who had lit the stick of dynamite. And he wasn't about to back off. Sakir wasn't a man for playtime in serious matters. Sure, he'd given her some leeway here, but he was starting to bristle, his full mouth thinning in unmasked irritation.

She had little choice but to confess. "I needed to get my sister, Ava, and my niece back here to Paradise."

Sakir crossed his arms over his broad chest. "For what purpose?"

"For…well, romantic purposes."

"Romance?"

The word rolled over his tongue with smooth sensuality, and Rita's skin tightened in response. "To rekindle an old flame—Ava's first and only love. This…this wedding was the only way I could get her home, get her daughter to finally meet her father." She shrugged. "Well, it seemed like the only way."

"I see," he said.

She gestured at him flippantly. "Then you had to show up." *Looking all tall, dark, handsome and impassive.*

He gave a bark of laughter. "Your fiancé should come to his wedding, should he not?"

"Don't look so smug, Sakir, okay? There wasn't supposed to be any wedding or any fiancé. He was imaginary. I just had to pick a guy, any guy."

"But it was not any *guy* that you picked, was it Rita?"

He took a step toward her, close enough for her to feel the heat off his body. "No."

"Did you stop to consider what the people of this town would think of me when I did not come? When I left a woman at altar?"

Rita stilled, heard his query once again in her mind. Shame enveloped her. No, she hadn't thought of what the townspeople would think. She hadn't thought of anything or anyone but her sister and niece.

She glanced over at the waiting crowd, several groups of them huddled together talking, their expressions perplexed. "No, I didn't think of how the town would react."

"I thought not."

"I didn't think of them and I didn't think of you." She faced him, totally sincere. "I'm sorry."

He nodded. "I accept your apology."

She paused. "You do?"

"Yes."

"That was quick."

"I do not believe in making one suffer for her transgressions."

That was big of him, Rita thought. But after all she had done, his manner was a little suspect. She asked, "You're not going to fire me?"

"No."

A wave of unease moved through her. "But that can't be why you're here, why you stood up there in front of all those people—just to get an apology out of me."

"No, I confess it is not."

"Was it revenge, then?" she asked through nervous laughter.

"I have something to ask of you, Rita," he said slowly.

"Okay." Unease suddenly morphed to apprehension.

"I have a business proposition."

"Business?" She glanced over her shoulder at the waiting crowd. This was madness—standing here with her mock fiancé, discussing business. Lord, how could she have let things get so out of control? How would she explain herself to her friends and family? "Can this business venture of yours wait? I need to get back and try to explain this mess to my guests."

"No, it cannot wait," Sakir said tightly.

"All right, what is it?"

He inhaled sharply, raised his chin. "First, I must ask if you are interested in a partnership. A temporary partnership in marriage for a permanent partnership in my business."

Rita's mouth dropped open.

"I offer you partnership in Al-Nayhal Corporation," he continued, "for staying married to me for three weeks' time."

"You're nuts." She gave a choked little laugh. Her voice hoarse, she cleared her throat, then began again. "You've got to be kidding."

"Do I ever 'kid,' Rita?"

She just stared at him. "No."

"I must go to my homeland for three weeks, and I need you there with me as my wife. Your…little plan here has given me the idea. Marriage shows stability, reliability, and this—though it is of no interest to me—is important for the businessmen in my country."

Rita listened, half expecting him to say, "I have made a joke. Yes, there is a first time for everything," but he never did. He kept going, kept explaining…

"I have been asked to come, to consult on the oil fields in Emand. I want this task to be done perfectly and I will go to any lengths to make sure that happens."

She watched his handsome face darken, his green eyes burn with determination. "I don't get it. Why is it so important to you?"

The passion dropped away, and possessiveness took its place. "That is my own affair."

"But you're making it mine, Sakir."

"When we return from Emand, the marriage can be dissolved, no harm to anyone—and you will become my equal."

She arched a brow at him. "Excuse me?"

"You understand my meaning."

She didn't understand any of this. "This is crazy. Listen, if making a show of marriage is that important to you, I could go with you as your pretend wife. I certainly owe you that much after this fiasco. But it doesn't have to be legal."

"For the people of my country, it must be."

He was completely and utterly serious. "How would they ever know?"

His eyes were shuttered. "My brother will know."

"You have a brother?"

He didn't respond. "Do you accept this offer?"

Did she accept this offer? She mentally rolled her eyes. She'd have to be mad to accept such an offer. Marriage for three weeks to a man she didn't love for partnership in his company.

…and she didn't like the way that last part sounded.

But then again… Then again, there was a part of her that wanted so desperately to travel, to experience a different kind of life, perhaps to lie in Sakir's bed and have him see her as a real woman for once. That part of her was shrieking the word *yes* inside her muddled brain.

"There's no marriage license—" she began.

"I have procured one."

"What? How—" She sniffed, shook her head. "Forget it, I know how." Money and power could make anything happen.

"Make no mistake regarding my intentions, Rita." He studied her face. "This is strictly business. I swear to you. No touch—" his jaw tightened "—no intimacies—"

"Right." It was strictly business on his part. She released a weighty breath. Well, of course it was. He had a job to do and as usual he'd called on his faithful assistant to help. Plain and simple.

"So, you agree, then?" he asked.

Why the hell not, she thought. She wanted to make partner. She wanted to travel. She wanted to get out of Paradise, and this was just three weeks of work—as usual. "All right."

He nodded. "Good."

She didn't wait to shake hands on the deal. She turned away and started up the easy hill toward the guests and waiting preacher. But suddenly, she paused and glanced over her shoulder. "I must warn you, as my *husband* and all, when I'm out of the office and not your assistant, I can be a little hard to handle."

A hint of amusement gleamed in his green eyes. "I know this. But like you, I have never shied away from a challenge."

Three

He was no proponent of marriage.

To Sakir, the thought of being held, captured or owned made him see red. But the idea of losing the biggest contract of his career, a contract that stemmed from his home country no less, had him seeing nothing but the victory and retribution he'd desired for far too many years.

He nodded to the preacher and said, "I will," then without being instructed to, leaned in and gave his beautiful assistant a quick kiss on the mouth.

It had to be quick, he knew. The woman tempted him far too much to give in to slow and deep and wet. And after all, he had given her his word to remain impassive.

With a calm smile, he took Rita's hand and led her back up the aisle as the crowd cheered and threw rose petals. Sakir chuckled. Just ten minutes ago, these people had been wearing expressions of unease, perhaps even pity, for they had thought the bride ready to call off her wedding.

She had not.

She had indeed married him.

As they walked toward the Lodge, Sakir took Rita's hand. He found it cold and shaky. What she had done was just dawning on her. Now she had to face her friends and family, lie about why she had taken her fiancé down to the water's edge and pretend that she was deeply in love. It was no easy feat.

Within seconds of them stepping inside the colorfully decorated Lodge, Rita was whisked away by several women. From the back of the Lodge, Sakir watched as she was urged into throwing her bouquet, grinned as she toyed with the excited females, laughing uproariously, until she finally turned around and hurled the flowers over her shoulder and into the waiting crowd.

"Fine day, isn't it, son?"

Son. Sakir bristled, turned and saw Rita's father walking toward him. He would *not* tell the man that not even his own father called him something so familiar, for he suspected that Ben Thompson was just looking for some sense of familiarity with a proud groom he had never met before.

Sakir inclined his head. "After a somewhat stilted beginning, the day is looking very fine indeed."

Ben grinned knowingly, then stuck out his hand. "For a minute there I thought all was lost."

Sakir shook the man's hand. "As did I."

"Well, it's good to finally meet you. When you didn't show up to my prenuptial lunch this week, I wanted to tan your hide—even with you being royalty and all. Then today when I didn't see you standing beside the preacher—well, you can imagine what was going through my mind."

"Yes."

"But all's well that ends well, eh? What'd she say to you down by the water? She can be pretty stubborn when she wants to be. Did she ask you to give up your throne or—"

"Dad." A beautiful blonde came up beside them, the shape of her eyes and mouth so similar to that of his bride.

"What is it, daughter?" Ben asked.

"The minister is waiting to speak to you. You have to get ready to make the toast."

"Right. Right." Ben shrugged, shook Sakir's hand again. "Well, congratulations, son—that's all I'm saying. You're a lucky man."

Sakir nodded. "I believe so."

When they were alone, the woman turned to Sakir and smiled. "I'm Ava, Rita's sister."

"Ah, yes, it is good to meet you."

"You, too." She hesitated for a moment, something on her mind, no doubt. Then, she said, "Look, my sister and I are really close. We love each other very much."

"It is good to care for one's siblings." He knew he must acknowledge as much, but the words were bitter on his tongue.

"I think so." She lowered her voice, leaned in just a little. "I know what she did for me, and I know what she's doing for you."

Surprise sliced through Sakir's easy manner "She has told—"

"Don't worry," Ava said quickly. "She just told me. Everyone thinks you're a happily married couple who had a few things to work out before they got hitched."

"Well, the last part is true, certainly."

"I just want to thank you."

"For what?"

She shrugged, her eyes sparkled. "Being a gentleman about Rita's little ruse. You could've really embarrassed her if you wanted to."

"As you said, she is doing me a favor as well."

Again, Ava shrugged, and softly said, "I hope you both get what you want out of this."

"No more than I."

She bit her lip. "Just do me a favor, okay?"

"Of course. If I can."

"Take care of her. She's wonderful and funny and loyal. She is a treasure to me and I don't want to see her get—"

Sakir put his hand over hers. "She is all of these things, and I will care for her."

Ava smiled. "That's all I wanted to hear." She walked away and called over her shoulder, "Have a great honeymoon, brother."

Again, with the familiarity. Sakir sighed. "We are not going on—" he began, then stopped short, the people around him staring.

"We're not going on what?" Rita came up beside him, a piece of wedding cake in her hands.

Sakir didn't say anything, just let his gaze roam over her foolishly and covetously. If he were ever to truly marry, if he were to ever believe in such a state, he would wish for his bride to be like Rita. In looks and in manner and in intelligence. She was all the things her sister had said and more.

Yet, to him, Rita would always have to remain untouchable.

She grinned at him, accepted his lack of reply and held up the plate of cake. "Before we have our first dance, we both need to eat some of this."

"Why?" White cake with thick white icing was not his idea of a sweet celebration.

"It's good luck," she said, then proceeded to take a small bite.

"I do not believe in luck."

"Well, I do. And we need as much as we can get with what we're about to do—so eat up." And with that, she took a piece of the cake and thrust it into his mouth.

Four

With wide, eager eyes, Rita gazed out of the tiny window into the dark night. "Well, this is some ride you got here, Sakir."

Now casually dressed in black pants and a black cashmere sweater, Sakir glanced up from his goat cheese salad and rack of lamb and gave her a nod. "Thank you. I find it very comfortable."

A silly laugh erupted from Rita's throat. *Comfortable.* That didn't really seem the appropriate term for a million-dollar Learjet with tan leather seating, matching carpets, mahogany cabinetry, a marble bathroom and a luxurious bedroom suite.

No, insanely awesome was far more appropriate.

"And to think," Rita said with a mock sigh of melancholy, "I could've been flying around to meet clients in this instead of tooling all over town in my Chevy Suburban."

"Your work keeps you in the office on most occasions."

She smiled widely. "Well, not anymore."

Sakir inclined his head. "No, not anymore."

Contemplatively, Rita returned to her meal. Here she was married to Sakir, sipping champagne and eating this fancy dinner aboard a private plane, when just hours ago she'd been back at the Paradise Lake Lodge bidding fond farewells to her sister, father and all the guests.

Totally surreal.

Yet absolutely the most exciting adventure of her life.

She took a sip of champagne and grinned as the bubbles tickled her nose. For three weeks, she was Sakir's wife. This gorgeous man whom she had fantasized about for years—used as her ideal in a marriage that was never intended to come off—was her lawfully wedded husband. Her smile faded a touch as she looked down at the plain gold band on the fourth finger of her left hand and recalled the "fine print" of this marriage. *It was only a business arrangement, a way to gain clients.* If she knew what was best for her, she'd do well to remember that.

She turned to Sakir and proceeded to look him over. So dark, so dangerous and so delicious in his black pants, black sweater and black mood. Resisting the urge to fling herself at him was going to be near impossible.

Boy, was she in trouble.

She pushed all thoughts of intimacy into the back of her mind and forced on a light façade. "I can't believe I was bargained into this marriage."

Sakir sniffed. "And I cannot believe I had to resort to such foolishness for an oil contract."

"Why did you, then?"

He returned to his meal and said nothing.

"Is impressing the folks back home worth all this?" she asked.

He looked up. Annoyance hovered in his eyes. "I am not looking to impress."

"No? Then what?"

"This is the 'hard to handle' you were speaking of, yes?" he asked drily.

She grinned. "Pretty much."

His expression was inscrutable, but a glimmer of heat swam in the depths of his eyes. "I was hoping it would surface in a much more pleasurable way."

A shudder of awareness moved through Rita. Maybe it was the craziness of the day or the fact that he was traveling to his homeland, but never in all the time she'd known Sakir had he said anything remotely like that. Teasing and just a little bit sexual. She had no idea what to say.

But in seconds, the look was gone and so was the casual manner. Control ruled Sakir's gaze again. "It is late," he said. "We have a long flight. I think it is best for you to rest now."

"I'm fine."

He continued as though he hadn't heard her. "I will remain here. I have much work to finish. Please—" he gestured at the door behind her "—take the suite."

Heat rushed into her cheeks. His suite? His bed? "I don't think so."

"It is very comfortable."

"I'm sure it is." And terrific torture for a woman with a massive crush.

Sakir looked very stiff and formal sitting in his leather captain's chair. "We have an agreement, Rita, and I would not break this agreement, no matter how…fatigued I become."

Rita's shoulders drooped and she suddenly felt weary. Of course he wouldn't. No matter how into him *she* was, Sakir just wasn't attracted to her. And never would be. His teasing manner had meant nothing, and she would do well to remember that in the future.

"All right." She stood up and moved to the door.

"One moment, Rita."

She turned around. "Yes?"

"I wish to thank you."

"For what?"

"Making this trip with me. It has been many years since I have been back to Emand. It will be a strange homecoming."

Sakir clipped her a nod, then returned to his meal, seemingly unaffected. But Rita was sure she'd seen a trace of vulnerability flashing in those green eyes—a foreign emotion to the cool sheikh, she assumed—and couldn't help but be intrigued.

He stared at his work, seeing nothing but a jumble of lines and shapes that seemed to be forming the outline of a woman on a bed.

With a growl of frustration, Sakir tossed the papers

aside and reached for the little gold case on the table beside him. He rarely indulged in fine cigars, but the special blend of herbs that came from his country called to him now as he imagined Rita slipping out of her clothes and crawling into his bed.

He lit the thin cheroot, inhaled deeply and relaxed back in his chair, as outside the plane's thick window the black night flashed by.

He was going home.

After too many years incommunicado, he was not entirely sure what to expect. No doubt, his brother would scorn him, but that mattered little. Sakir wanted only to win this account and, in the process, prove to his eldest brother, the reigning crown prince of Emand, that he had been mistaken in thinking Sakir wouldn't amount to anything outside his country.

Sakir switched off the overhead lights, sat in the darkness and watched the smoke from his cigar drift upward toward the vent, making the shape of a woman's curves.

She slept in his bed, between his sheets.

His wife.

He shook his head, took another drag of his cigar. She was not his wife. She was his business associate.

No woman would claim him that way.

Since leaving Emand, Sakir had become cold and hard—in body and in spirit. He wanted only to be immersed in his work and to build an empire of his own. When his body ached, he took a lover, but he gave himself to no woman.

In his mind's eye, he saw Rita and felt her mouth beneath his as he kissed her once, quickly and without passion, at the altar. She had wanted more; he knew the taste of desire on a woman's lips—and, God help him, he had wanted to give it to her. But he would not. He had grown to depend on her and he was not about to allow his desire to overshadow his responsibilities.

His manservant entered quietly. "Do you need anything, Your Highness?"

The woman who lay sleeping in his bed.

"No."

When his servant left, Sakir took another drag of his cigar and reveled in the peace of the darkness.

Five

The Emand airport buzzed with activity. Tourists and locals bandied about looking for luggage and unoccupied taxis, while airport personnel shouted at them for not having the proper tickets and identification.

But for Rita Thompson, or rather Rita Al-Nayhal, things were far simpler. Meeting her and Sakir at their private gate were ten guards and four attendants, all ready to do as the sheikh and his wife bid them.

Within ten minutes of landing, she and Sakir were whisked out of the airport and deposited in separate limousines. Rita had little time to be shocked, not to mention annoyed, by the strange gesture, because in seconds the door to her limousine opened and Sakir stepped inside, wearing a white caftan with gold trim and a staid expression on his handsome face.

An enormous guard with wide brown eyes and olive skin stood in the doorway. "Your Highness, this isn't wise."

"I did not ask for any of this, Fandal," Sakir said, irritation threading his voice. "I did not come to Emand on ceremony."

"Yes, Your Highness, I understand this, but you see His Royal Highness—"

Sakir shot the large man a look so paralyzing he actually took a step back. "I see only that my brother has a hand in this. And I do not accept." Sakir reached out, grabbed the handle and shut the door.

"Drive on," he commanded the chauffeur.

Rita watched Sakir as they took off down the city streets. His face showed little emotion as he seized several documents from his briefcase and began to study them. In his offices in Texas, Sakir was a serious and intense businessman, granted; but in his country, he seemed rigid. He looked as though he needed to lighten up a little before he cracked in the desert heat.

"You know, I'm really flattered, Sakir," Rita said, her tone relaxed, almost playful.

"Why is that?"

"Well, you wanted to ride in *my* car and not one of your own."

He glanced up from his work, his gaze impassive. "It is tradition for royalty to ride separate from their family."

She grinned broadly. "I like a man who breaks with tradition."

A hint of a smile ruffled his sensuous mouth and his eyes softened—just a touch. "I ride here with you because I must make a statement to my family. I am no longer one of them."

"A member of the family or a royal?"

"Both."

"You might reject that notion, Sakir, but look at this." She gestured about. "Limo, private plane, bodyguards— I'm afraid you'll always be a prince."

A muscle twitched in his jaw. "I may have been born to this life, Rita, but I am not a part of it. Not anymore."

"Does that mean I won't be meeting your brother?" she asked as outside the desert landscape whizzed by.

"I imagine you will meet him."

He didn't sound pleased about the introduction and Rita couldn't help but wonder what in the world had happened between Sakir and his family that had driven him out of Emand and driven the people closest to him out of his heart.

"Do you have other family besides your brother?" she asked.

"I have a nephew."

She was surprised. "Your brother's married?"

"No. He fathered a child. The woman did not want the boy, she wanted financial freedom instead."

"How horrible."

Sakir didn't agree or disagree, just explained. "Zayad gave her riches in exchange for his child."

Rita couldn't imagine such a thing. "Your brother sounds like a good man."

Sakir's eyes darkened, as did his mood. "Perhaps we should talk of protocol now."

"Getting too personal, am I?" she said in jest, determined to keep the mood as light as possible.

"You are." Sakir gave her a dangerous smile, his gaze intense. "But I was prepared for personal."

Butterflies in the belly, she thought drily. Well, she hadn't felt that in years. "You were saying something about protocol?"

He nodded. "You are my wife, Rita. This does not mean the same here as it does in America."

"Is this about my clothes," she asked, smoothing down her blue silk dress. "Do I need to be wearing something more traditional?"

"No. You look—" he paused, his gaze moving over her, slowly, intently "—very beautiful. The color of your dress is magnificent with your eyes."

She felt her cheeks warm. "Thank you."

His gaze remained fixed. "No, this is about behavior."

She laughed with piqued amusement. "I'm not curtsying or kissing your feet or anything, Sakir, so you can just forget it."

"There will be no curtsying."

"Good to know."

He shot her a penetrating stare. "And I would never ask you to kiss my feet, Rita."

Heat coiled within her at his gaze. How did he do it? How did he make her weak and wanting with one look? It wasn't fair.

"What are you asking of me, then?" she asked.

"I would wish for you to treat me with respect, that is all."

"Of course. And you will do the same?"

He nodded.

Rita's gaze suddenly shifted out the window and to the view of a lifetime. Breath rushed out of her lungs. "Holy cow."

"What is wrong?"

"Wrong?" She pointed past him. "Look at that. I've never seen such an amazing hotel."

Surely Aladdin must've asked the genie in the lamp to conjure him up such a place, Rita thought, completely stunned. Situated high on a rugged desert landscape, with mountains behind it, sat an enormous fortress. Domes and balconies stretched high into the cloudless blue, the exterior brilliant in shades of gold and terracotta. "It's like something out of a fairy tale," Rita said with deep awe threading her voice.

Sakir didn't even glance over his shoulder. "That is not a hotel."

"What? It's got to be—"

"That is my family home, Rita."

She turned, stared at him. "You're kidding?"

"No."

"But it's so beautiful and…"

"And?"

She laughed. "Well, enormous for such few to live there."

He shrugged. "It is comfortable."

She laughed again, this time at his apathy. "Just like the plane, right?"

"Yes."

She shook her head. "I don't get it. You left all of this for Texas?"

His gaze remained shuttered. "I left what is inside."

Curiosity curled within her. His words were so daunting, so mysterious. More than anything in the world, she wanted to know what had happened here, happened to him and his family. But she seriously doubted that Sakir would ever share his past history with her. He was far too proud a man to let her see his scars, emotional or otherwise.

But she could, perhaps, scratch the surface.

"There's something I don't understand, Sakir," she said.

"What?"

"You don't want to be a part of this—of this royal life—yet we're staying in the palace?"

He sighed. "I would not wish it. There are many places for us to stay. But for our clients, I'm afraid the palace is the only option. They are traditional. They would not understand my staying at a hotel when my family is here. Their trust in me would be compromised."

"So you're willing to toss out your principles for this deal?"

Sudden anger lit his eyes. "Do not speak to me of principles. Was it not you who fabricated an entire ceremony for the sake of your sister?"

"That's different."

"How?"

"It was a sacrifice. For her happiness."

"You lied to many. Principles were tossed out, yes?"

"Yes, okay." She shifted in her seat, faced him dead on. "So who are you making happy in this deal besides yourself, Sakir?"

His nostrils flared. "You could not possibly understand."

"No, I think I understand pretty well," she countered. She knew in her gut that he was back for more than scoring a major business deal, though she was pretty sure he wouldn't acknowledge that fact.

"I see you wish to debate, Rita. And on most occasions I would be pleased to accommodate you." His cool stare drilled into her. "But not today."

"Fine." Rita said nothing else, just eased back against the seat and watched Sakir's family home grow closer. She wouldn't push him for more—not right now. He had demons to wrestle with, a history she didn't know anything about, and he had a right to his privacy.

For now.

They drove through three gates, each with several armed guards until finally they rolled up into a circular drive. A man waited at the top of the steps, handsome and almost familiar in his looks and manner. He wore a crisp white caftan and stood with his hands behind his back, very tall and proud as he watched the car approach.

Fandal, the olive-skinned uniformed servant who resembled an oak tree, opened the door, bowed low. "Your Highness."

"He was not to be here," Sakir hissed at the man as he stepped out of the car.

"He insisted, Your Highness."

Sakir said no more. He helped Rita out of the limousine and then walked up the steps.

"Hello, Zayad," Sakir said, his tone cool and his hand outstretched.

Zayad grasped his hand. "Hello, brother. It has been a long time."

Sakir nodded, then turned to Rita. "I would like to introduce you to—"

"Your wife. Yes, I know." Zayad grinned at Rita, then reached for her hand. "A pleasure."

"It's nice to meet you, Your Highness."

"Zayad, please." The handsome man with intense black eyes bent and kissed her hand. "After all, we are family now."

Rita smiled. "Thanks for having us, Zayad."

"You are most welcome." He turned and motioned for them to follow him up the beautiful marble steps and into the palace. "You are a lucky man, Sakir. If I could only find a woman as beautiful as your Rita, perhaps I would take a wife myself."

Sakir didn't reply, but his arm snaked around Rita's waist. "Are our rooms ready?"

"They are."

"Good."

The hall they entered was spectacular. It had gilded coffered ceilings with geometric moldings and landscape murals on the walls. Rita simply stared, her eyes widening as she took in the red marble floor that stretched out to meet a gold staircase.

Zayad gave them an easy smile. "I'm sure you would like to relax and perhaps take some refreshment."

"We would," Sakir said.

"Gana will take you to your apartments, then." Zayad inclined his head before turning to leave. "I will see you both at supper."

Sakir's voice boomed through the hall after his brother. "We will take our meal in our rooms as you must be busy."

With a chuckle, Zayad didn't turn, but called back, "Not tonight, Sakir. Not tonight."

Rita could feel the stiff annoyance of the man beside her and she reached for his hand. But Sakir moved away, clearly not able to accept her comfort.

A petite, dark-haired woman—very pretty and in her mid-twenties—bowed low and said nothing, but motioned for them to follow her.

They ascended the gold staircase and walked down a long hallway that sported several balconies, heavy with flowers and plants. The warm, jasmine-scented breeze wafted in through the open balcony doors, reminding Rita that she was in a foreign land—traveling and exploring for the first time in her life.

She smiled, said to Sakir, "Your brother's very charming."

"Yes," Sakir said drily. "Women tend to fall in love with him at first sight, so I would ask that you remember you are my wife for the next three weeks. After that, you may do as you wish."

She tossed Sakir a wry glance. "Is that anger or jealousy in your tone, Sakir? I can't tell."

"It is neither," he muttered, though a nerve jumped in his jaw.

Rita smiled as she followed Gana into the rooms she and Sakir would be staying in for their three weeks of marriage. But her smile quickly faded as the room came into view. It was far too grand for a simple girl from a small ranching town in Texas, that was for sure.

The large living area was both opulent and warm. Painted in pale green and gold, it had an almost Asian flair, with Chinese tapestries and furnishings inlaid with mother-of-pearl.

"This is extraordinary," Rita said, walking from the living area into a massive bedroom, which boasted a painted domed ceiling, royal-blue silk bed linens and a gold-encrusted canopy.

Rita stopped short. "Ah, Sakir?"

"Yes?"

She turned, saw him in the doorway of the bedroom, his green eyes burning with amusement.

"There's one bed," she said.

"I see that."

Her heart tripped. "I understand that we need to keep up pretenses—"

"We are married, Rita."

Was it her imagination, or did his gaze caress her? Was it her imagination, or was he implying that they sleep together for their own enjoyment and not because they were thrown together through a business deal?

"And it is a rather large bed." His mouth was so firm, so sensual.

Heat pooled in Rita's belly, then snaked lower.

He grinned. "Of course, I can sleep on the floor if that would make you more comfortable."

Why was she so nervous? She was attracted to Sakir and had fantasized about sleeping with him. Rita swallowed hard, opened her mouth to say something, anything; she could barely think.

But before she could get one word out, Gana appeared beside Sakir, her gaze lowered. "Your Highness?"

Rita looked expectantly at Sakir, who in turn grinned at her and said, "She is speaking to you, Rita."

"Oh," she said, suddenly a little flustered. She smiled at the young woman. "I'm sorry."

Gana looked up shyly. "Will you follow, Your Highness?"

"Of course." Rita walked past Sakir, then paused. "Will I see you later or—"

His eyes burned with intensity as he said, "You will see me soon."

Attempting to mentally cool her heated skin under such a gaze, Rita took a deep breath and followed Gana into a lavish changing room. There were gold accents and polished antique Chinese porcelain everywhere.

"I have drawn a bath for you, Your Highness," she said.

The ever-present "Your Highness" title was slowly bringing Rita back to, well, reality—if that were even possible here. Especially as the pretty young woman before her started to remove Rita's clothing—a very strange feeling, as no one had undressed her since her mother. And that had ended sometime around the second grade.

But Rita didn't fight with the woman. She was here in this exotic, fantasy world for only three weeks. No matter what oddities turned up, she was going to go with the flow and hopefully have an interesting, educational and fabulous time in the process.

After Gana helped her into a lovely silk robe, she led Rita into a large, pale blue marble bathroom with high ceilings, French doors leading out to a terrace and two dark blue marble tubs, each the size of a small swimming pool.

Rita sucked in a breath at the vision before her, her mouth suddenly dry as the desert outside the open windows.

Rose petals skimmed the surface of one bath, while her gorgeous sheikh husband skimmed the surface of the other.

Six

She wore the cream silk robe he'd chosen for her, Sakir noticed, a lethal combination of pride and savage desire rising up to claim him as he reclined in the bath.

Just two days ago, he had glimpsed through several books brought to him by his personal shopper. Books of fine women's clothing from all of the best houses in Paris and Milan. Granted, Rita owned many fine business suits, he knew, but she had little clothing that befitted a woman of her rank.

A princess of Emand.

Sakir let his gaze travel over her like a starving man. The pale silk clung to her hips like a lover's hands. Her waist, small and supple, begged to be encircled. And her full breasts swelled pink and enticing beneath the gaping fabric at her chest.

It was a good thing he sat in deep water, Sakir mused, as the lower half of his body was hard as the marble that surrounded him.

With a cool smile, Sakir motioned toward the pool. "The water is warm and scented with herbs."

She glanced down at the water, then back up. She raised a brow at him.

"Please join me, Rita."

Surprise remained steadfast in her eyes. "I think I'll wait for my bath until later."

"I have never known you to be shy," he said.

"Only in certain naked situations." She gave a smart little laugh. "I've been pretty busy lately—"

"Planning a wedding?"

"Right," she continued on quickly. "So I haven't been working out all that much. No crunches or leg lifts. And don't get me started on the chocolate addiction that's taken over my life."

Sakir slowly smiled. "I am quite certain that what dwells beneath your silk robe is a paradise that needs no apology."

Rita's mouth dropped open and two splashes of pink stained her cheeks.

Sakir was a little surprised at the bold compliment that had slipped so easily from his lips, but he did not retreat. He grinned at her, his brow lifted. "But I will keep my eyes averted, if that would make you more comfortable."

Rita snorted at this. "Not sure anything's going to

make me feel comfortable at this point. I'll take a rain check, Sakir."

Behind Rita, Gana entered quietly, her arms laden with fresh towels. She was too fine a servant to show her confusion at the scene before her, but Sakir detected something behind her dark eyes. Perhaps she was wondering why a wife would still be clothed and dry before her husband. Her husband the sheikh…

Sakir leaned back against the cool marble. It would not do to have Gana telling tales to his brother's manservant about problems within Sakir's marriage. His mission here was too important.

"Wife," Sakir began, using a tone he'd heard last from his deceased father. "I command you to join me."

Rita's gaze shifted from apprehensive to savage blue fire in seconds. "Excuse me?"

Sakir glanced pointedly at Gana, back at Rita, then lifted his brow.

Rita's lips thinned, clearly understanding his meaning, but she refused to budge.

"I would ask that you obey me at once."

"Obey you?" she fairly growled.

"Rita…"

Eyes narrowed with annoyance, Rita muttered the word, "Fine."

In a great show of importance, Sakir put his hands behind his head, took a deep breath, smiled and waited for what would come next.

Rita, on the other hand, looked stiff as a poker as she reached for the edges of her silk robe. "I can't believe this," she muttered. She bit her lip; then, suddenly, she stopped and gave Sakir an acerbic smile. "Averting the eyes would be good now, Your Highness."

His grin widened and he dropped his gaze to the bathwater before him. "As you wish, my love."

The first sound he heard was her snort of derision. The second sound was the tantalizing whisper of silk hitting tile. And the third, the soft splash of nude, pink curves meeting warm, scented water.

Sakir felt tense, on edge with need.

No doubt he would be damned for all eternity, but he could not help himself—his gaze flickered upward.

Only a brief glimpse of her smooth belly and the soft curve of her breast were his.

And only for a moment.

But it was enough to cause him great torment in mind and body.

He released an impatient breath. Only a moment ago, he had plied Rita with silly compliments about what was beneath her robe. Never could he have imagined how just a taste of that vision would send him reeling with a desire he'd never known.

"Thank you, Gana," he heard Rita say. "You can go. We're good from here."

Sakir glanced up just in time to see the young servant's back as she walked out the bathroom door. And just in time to find Rita glaring at him.

"We're alone now, Your Highness," she said, her tone threaded with ire. "Any other commands you wish to give me?"

The question gave him pause, as he saw himself lying beneath her, commanding her to take whatever she wished from him, whatever would please her. A very impractical and foolish vision, he concluded. "I apologize for my brutish behavior, but I am afraid it was a necessity."

"I sure hope so, because that was completely humiliating."

"I do not see how."

"Oh, really?" She waved her arm at him and lowered her voice, "'I command you, wife.' Not something you hear everyday around Paradise—or want to hear for that matter."

He chuckled. He could not help himself. She was so spirited. And…correct. "You did bring this on yourself, you know."

"How's that? I just thought I was taking a bath after a long flight."

"You agreed to be the wife of a sheikh. This comes with certain…expectations."

"And you agreed to mutual respect," she countered.

Sakir paused, thought about this and then nodded. "True. You are right."

"Again," she said, her eyes brightening with a tinge of amusement.

"Do not push matters," Sakir said, his chin lifted. "But yes."

She smiled. "And you apologize?"

"Perhaps."

Rita felt the fight in her ease somewhat. Getting a man to admit he was wrong was a pretty tough task, but with Sakir such admissions were rare. She shrugged, her smile broadening. "You're forgiven."

"Very good."

With all the talk of propriety and apology, Rita had forgotten for a moment that she was naked, in very clear water and close to Sakir. Feeling a little too exposed, she reached for a cluster of fragrant herbs and steered them toward her chest.

"Oh, and Rita?"

She glanced up. "Yes, Sakir?"

"You have nothing to be ashamed of."

He sat there, staring at her—dangerous, sexy, his skin so dark and threaded with sinewy muscle.

She swallowed tightly. "What do you mean?"

His gaze dipped. "Your body is quite beautiful."

Her pulse skittered alarmingly. "You promised you'd look away."

He shrugged. "Normally, I am a man of my word, but—"

"Not today?"

His full mouth twitched with amusement. "I am afraid not. I am afraid the temptation was too great."

"I don't understand you, Your Highness."

"What is it you do not understand?"

"Back in Texas you were Mr. Straight-laced, Mr. Reserved, Mr. Concealed, Mr.—"

"I understand, Rita, please go on."

"Well, now look at you." She gestured at him.

"What is it you see?" he asked with a smooth, sensual grin.

Her stomach flipped over. Literally, flipped. "You've been home for an hour and you're so…you're…" The words—*relaxed, teasing, on fire*—died on her lips as Sakir calmly and coolly stood up and stepped out of the bath totally and utterly naked.

"I am what?" he asked.

Through the haze of desire that leapt from brain to breasts to belly, she came up with just two words to that query.

My fantasy.

Not an appropriate response, but oh, so true.

Sakir stood there, above her, before her, resplendent, and she allowed her gaze to travel the length of him. His calves were hard and finely muscled; his thighs were lean and toned; his buttocks were sculpted and curved in at the sides.

And then there was his pride. Long, pink and hard.

Heat snaked through her heavy, tight body, and her breathing fell labored. She'd never thought such things in her life. And in such a way. It was being here, in this land of spice and decadent sunsets, that had her conjuring such descriptions. It had to be.

"I will dress now," he said.

"Good idea," she muttered.

"I will send Gana to assist you. We have dinner in thirty minutes' time."

He didn't take a towel. Just walked back into the dressing area, his broad, tan back glistening with bathwater.

Rita inhaled deeply, her body wound tight as a drum.

She was in serious trouble.

With a meek little whimper, she plugged her nose and sank beneath the herb-scented water.

A half hour later, Rita stood in front of her bedroom mirror and smiled at what she saw. Exquisite blue and green silk encircled her torso and pooled at her feet. True, the dress covered her far more than what she was used to, but with the many beautiful items of clothing Gana had laid out for her, the traditional Emand dress had seemed perfect for a dinner at the palace.

"Thank you."

Rita spun around, her heart in her throat. Just a few feet away, knee-bucklingly handsome in a white and gold caftan stood Sakir.

"Thanks for what?" she asked.

"Wearing that dress." He walked to her, his gaze searching hers. "I picked it out myself, but I did not expect that you would want to wear it."

"Why not?"

"In Emand, it is a fairly modern costume, but for an American woman—"

"Well, for this American woman, it's beautiful."

Sakir took her hand, brought it to his lips and kissed her palm. "You are beautiful, Rita."

Her heart thundered in her chest. From the bathwater to the bedroom, little had changed—in her feelings, at any rate.

Lord, she thought, drinking him in. What in the world did she do now? Could she tell him he was beautiful, too? That she loved his kiss? Could she ask him to move a little closer? Whisper to him that she'd take that very same kiss on her mouth, her neck, her shoulder?

Rita exhaled. What a crazy notion. He'd surely reject her. And she couldn't handle that—not right now. Maybe when she got back to Paradise and they were going their separate ways…but not now.

No, she'd just wait and see—and maybe hope a little, too—that Sakir's transformation from perfectly balanced boss into sexy suitor would continue.

She gave him a pleasant smile. "Thank you for the compliment."

Sakir nodded, placed her hand on his forearm and led her out of the room.

Silence fell between them as they walked down the elaborate hallway. Rita wondered if he was having some of the same thoughts she'd been having. But, of course, she wasn't about to ask. So instead, she racked her brain for some significant, yet light, conversation. "So, when you were a little boy did you run up and down these hallways like a maniac?"

Sakir turned, gave her a wry glance. "What do you think?"

Rita laughed. "To be honest, I can't imagine you as anything but a serious child, Sakir."

"I do not remember a time when I was not." He led her down the staircase. "Except…"

His voice trailed off and Rita tugged on his arm. "Go on."

"It is an uninteresting anecdote, to be sure."

"I'll be the judge of that."

Sakir snorted.

Rita laughed. "Don't you dare leave me hanging like that. I'll…"

"You will what?" He stopped at the bottom of the stairs and found her gaze.

She shrugged, said mysteriously, "I don't know, but whatever it is, you don't want to risk it."

"Perhaps I do."

Heat moved between them, solid and dangerous.

Rita fought for her voice, which was lost in the haze of desire that shrouded them both. "I want the story, Sakir."

A grin ruffled his full mouth. "All right. I did have a rather fervent desire for figs as a child. I would do just about anything to have them."

Now, this was interesting. "Really? Like what?"

He leaned close, whispered in her ear. "There was a night or two in which I scaled the palace walls and escaped into the dark night—"

"Good evening."

The mood had been heated, sensual and intimate, but the steely timbre of the sultan's voice brought a cold wind lashing between her and Sakir. They moved apart as Zayad walked toward them.

"I trust you had time to relax and recover from your trip?" he asked with all politeness.

"Yes, thanks," Rita said.

Zayad turned to Sakir. "And you, brother? I hope you have found some rest."

Rita watched Zayad, confused. Deep interest threaded his tone, as though he really cared about his brother's well-being. She had been under the impression that Sakir and Zayad were at odds with each other, but Zayad's manner, just as it had been when they'd arrived, didn't hold an ounce of antagonism.

Unlike Sakir's cold indifference, she noted.

"I would expect your staff has informed you of our every move, Zayad," Sakir said.

Zayad shook his head. "Still the cynic, brother?"

"A realist, I think."

Zayad said nothing, merely nodded and then beckoned for them to follow. They left the hall and walked through several exquisitely furnished rooms. There were silk tapestries and gold moldings, jeweled frames with artwork that clearly belonged in a museum and priceless crystal chandeliers.

It was a sight to behold.

"Here we are."

Before Rita sat a massive dining room, done in red silks and velvet, with luscious gold accents. The splendor and sumptuousness of the room were to be expected after seeing the rest of the house, but Rita still felt in awe of her surroundings. A royal palace, to be sure. Very different than her comfy little two-storey back home.

She was seated next to Sakir and across from Zayad at a table that could easily sit fifty. Candles burned cheerfully, and while the meal was served and the wine flowed, the conversation began.

"How long will you be staying?" Zayad asked.

After taking a healthy swallow of wine, Sakir said, "Three weeks."

"Is that all?"

"I am afraid so."

"Your wife and I will hardly be acquainted in such a short time." Zayad turned to Rita and smiled.

"Pity," replied Sakir, his tone as dry as the desert outside.

Zayad continued to focus on Rita, perhaps knowing he wouldn't be getting much out of Sakir tonight. "You once worked for Sakir, is that right?"

"She still does," Sakir said before Rita could answer.

Zayad raised a brow. "Is that so?"

Rita nodded, her mouth full of tomato and cucumber salad.

"Ah, partnership in business and in marriage," Zayad said. "How fulfilling."

"Yes." Sakir glanced at Rita, his eyes a strange combination of heat and impatience. "It can be that."

With a quick nod to his personal servant, Zayad's plate was filled with a luscious-looking beef dish. "Americans marry for love, do they not?" he asked Rita.

"Most do," Rita said, also accepting the fragrant meat.

"We were never afforded such a luxury, were we, brother?"

"No."

Rita smiled at Sakir. "Living abroad has its perks, doesn't it?"

A flicker of a grin touched his lips. "Indeed."

Zayad watched them, watched their interaction. "But you must pine for the desert of Joona, Sakir, and the waterfalls up north."

Sakir's jaw went tight as a trap. "I am content."

"Well then, I am happy for this. But there are others to consider."

Sakir said nothing and took another swallow of wine.

"The people of Emand—your people—have missed you." Zayad leaned back in his chair. "They are throwing a celebration in honor of your return. You and Rita, of course."

"What?" Sakir fairly snapped.

Zayad nodded. "Tomorrow. Noon. In the marketplace. It is tradition."

"I do not think—"

Zayad did not let him finish. "There would be much disappointment were you and Rita not to attend."

Rita watched Sakir—watched his hand curl around his wineglass in a death grip, watched his nostrils flare. "I would not disappoint the people of Emand, as you well know."

"I do know." Zayad lifted his brow. "So you will be there?"

"We will be there," Sakir said through gritted teeth.

Zayad nodded. "Good. I must leave you now. My son is calling from school and I would speak with him." He bowed to Rita. "It has been a pleasure. Good night."

Rita forced a smile. "'Night."

Zayad faced Sakir. "Brother."

Sakir said nothing, though his gaze never left his brother as the man walked out of the room.

"Well," Rita began. "What do we do now?"

Sakir took a long time in answering. "There is always work to be done."

"Yes, there is always work."

Rita sighed, feeling a little melancholy—not to mention a little confused about what had happened between her and Sakir in the hall earlier and, just now, between him and his brother. But getting answers out of her "husband" seemed like an impossible task right now.

"Have you finished your meal?" he asked.

"Yes."

He nodded, stood. "Good. Because there is something I wish to show you."

"Contracts or stats?" she asked with a soft chuckle.

"Neither." He offered her his hand. "We have gardens here that are purported to be hypnotic in their fragrance and beauty. I wish to see if this is still so."

The warmth that had dwelled within her earlier, in the tub and standing with Sakir in front of her mirror, returned. Smiling, she stood up and took his hand. "Well, a little hypnotizing sounds good."

Yes, it did, Sakir thought as he led Rita down the hall, toward the back of the house, through a massive open-air atrium and out into the night.

Anything to ease the tension that had surged through him at dinner, in the presence of his brother.

At the entrance to the grounds, he stopped and watched Rita as she took in all fifty-seven acres of magnificence. Or what he'd always referred to as his child-hood playground.

The thought made Sakir smile. He'd had a good childhood, for the most part.

"Wow," he heard Rita utter from beside him.

"What?"

She pointed to their right. Sunset was creeping si-lently into the rose gardens, with fingers of red and bur-nished orange hovering above the rare trees, shrubs, conifers and palms beyond.

Sakir released the breath he'd been holding since landing in Emand.

He was home.

Truly home.

Where the palace had always served as a watchful keeper, the gardens had been his sanctum.

"This is just amazing," Rita said.

"There is much to see," Sakir said, guiding her down the stone pathways to the medicinal gardens, rock wall and succulents.

"I feel as though I'm stepping into another time, as though this is sacred ground," she said with a lilt to her voice. "Does that sound crazy?"

"Not at all." Sakir led her over a bridge and toward one of the many glass atriums and lath houses that were used for indoor plants. "This garden was started thou-sands of years ago, so you are right about stepping into another time."

A perfectly kept stand of fruit trees followed, the tart scent of fresh lemons heavy in the air. Then orange and plum. It was like Eden. Yes, a true biblical setting, and Sakir wondered how many sins he was willing to commit to have the woman beside him.

"Let's stop for a moment," he suggested.

The sounds of the garden, the insects and the wind in the desert beyond filled the disquiet between them.

"Sakir," Rita said quietly.

"Yes?"

"Do you think your brother suspects that we're not…"

"Truly husband and wife?"

"Yes."

"I am not certain." At that, he turned to face her. His gut twisted violently. She was so beautiful, with her skin glowing in the light of the sunset and her eyes filled with a longing he knew all too well. "But I do think he believes we are lovers."

She looked surprised. "Why? We really don't show any signs of being lovers."

This brought a smile to Sakir's face. No doubt Zayad had seen Sakir's covetous manner and sensuous gaze whenever he looked at Rita.

"And what would those signs be, Rita?"

She smiled, her eyes dancing with amusement. "Looking at each other with desire in our eyes, bathing together, holding hands."

He grinned, his hands closing around hers as he moved closer to her.

She chuckled. "Now, if he'd have seen the kiss at our wedding, he'd have known we're not lovers."

"Yes, that was rather formal."

"Yeah, it was."

Without checking his actions, Sakir reached out and touched her cheek, his thumb brushing over her lower lip. "It was not the kiss I had intended."

She tipped her chin up. "Really?"

He shook his head slowly. "The kiss I had intended would not have been suitable for others to view." Sakir eased her into his arms. "Shall I show you?"

"Sakir…"

With his mouth inches from hers, he said, "You may tell me *no* at any time, Rita—tell me to release you."

She looked tormented and as on fire as he was. "There is no command this time?"

"Only from you."

"Then," she said, her breathing labored, "I want you to kiss me."

He smiled.

"We're breaking the rules…"

"Yes," he said before covering her mouth with his own.

Seven

Rita melted against him, her knees turning to water as every nerve in her body flooded with desire. In her mind, she'd imagined this—standing hip to hip with Sakir, her breasts crushed against his chest as he made love to her mouth with reckless abandon.

But nothing in her fantasy had prepared her for the decadence of reality.

Or with how highly skilled her fantasy lover truly was.

Sakir kissed her with severity, his passion desperate as his hands raked up her back, his fingers digging into her neck as he held her steady. Rita could do little but shiver and moan with the sweet force of his movement.

As the sunset turned to quiet twilight around them, Sakir turned Rita to liquid both inside and out, his tongue moving between her lips slowly, tasting her need. Then, when she'd had enough of his playful torture, when she'd whimpered and thrust her hips up against his erection, he feasted on her mouth once again.

He crushed her lips, then eased back into soft, wet kisses.

Rita moaned, her body begging for his—on top of her, beneath her, it didn't matter as long as they were naked and close.

Lord, it had been so long since a man had touched her this way, held her so tight that she felt his heart beating against her breasts. She'd almost forgotten what it felt like to be wanted.

Years ago, she'd given her body to a man she'd thought she was in love with. But her judgment had been skewed by hope and a young woman's romanticism. Her lover had used her for just one night and then dropped her flat. Something had closed around her heart that day. She'd allowed herself only fantasies since then.

Until now, that is.

Until Sakir.

As if hearing her thoughts, Sakir pulled her even closer, changing the angle of his kiss. His mouth felt so hot, so warm as he raked his hands down her back, down, down until he cupped her backside.

Rita whimpered. Her breasts tingled, and between her thighs a fire raged. She thrust her hips against him once more. She wanted to say, "Take me. Make love to me now before I melt right here." But she didn't want to move her mouth from his.

She hoped her body spoke for her.

But the only one to speak was Sakir. And his word was a muffled oath against her mouth.

"What?" she whispered, still deep in a passion-filled haze. "What's wrong?"

"We have company." Sakir straightened slowly, his eyes still on Rita, and still burning with danger and unquenched desire. "They will be upon us momentarily."

Breathlessly, Rita fought for her composure as she heard the sound of male laughter behind her.

"Maybe we should go inside?" Rita suggested, desperate to hold on to the heat of the moment. Yes, they could go upstairs—undress each other quickly, lie down in their bed, beneath those luscious silk sheets, and continue what they'd started here.

"Yes," Sakir said, his gaze shifting to the palace doors.

Rita reached for his hand, but he moved away. A chill moved through her.

"You are right," he said, a coolness to his tone as well. "Let us move inside. I fear I have neglected my work long enough."

It was as though a knife had been thrust into Rita's heart. Sakir had completely misinterpreted her suggestion. But if it was pointed or by accident, she didn't know. Though honestly, she didn't really want to know.

"I wasn't talking about work, Sakir." She tried once again to take his hand. "There's so much more to life than work, Sakir."

"Not for me," he said proudly, taking her hand and slipping it into his arm.

Rita felt herself nod. Her mind and body were floating somewhere between lust and shock; she fought for the light of reality. She knew she needed to see the truth here— that she'd just been rejected. Sure, she'd felt this kind of brush-off before, but with Sakir it felt so much worse.

A moment ago, he was making love to her mouth.

Sakir led her away from the lemon grove and toward the house. "I must apologize, Rita."

"What for?" she asked roughly, though she already knew the answer.

"I went too far, took things to a place they were never meant to go."

His words bit into her, but she remained poised. "I went there with you, Sakir."

"Yes, but there is a difference—"

She wouldn't let him finish. She stopped just outside the doorway and faced him, her chin lifted. "I enjoyed myself back there. I'm sorry you couldn't allow yourself to do the same."

A muscle under his eye twitched, his lips thinned. "You can find your way back to the suite? Or shall I escort—"

Rita shook her head. She wanted to be alone, feel her anger and frustration as she tried to figure out just what had really happened here. "No, I'll be fine. You get your work done."

She gave him zero chance for a comeback. Any more apologies, explanations or excuses and she'd get in a cab and head for the airport.

She walked into the house, away from her husband and the man she had an enormous crush on, and refused to look back. But as she took those steps, she realized that for the first time since she'd come to Emand, she wished she'd kept Sakir as a fantasy.

For the reality was becoming far too complicated.

The grounds, desert and city stretched out before him.

Sakir leaned against the balcony attached to his tower offices at the palace—the offices that had once belonged to his father—and breathed in the spiced scent of Emand and the fading warmth of the surrounding deserts. For many years, he had put this world and all of its memories to rest. He had put aside the notion of family and, in return, had become a cool, sharp and impassive businessman.

But things were starting to shift.

Ever since he had stepped off the plane today onto the soil of his homeland, that impassive shield had begun to slip.

The lights of the city began to flicker on and the sight made him smile, though he couldn't stop the deep ache of homesickness that filled him.

He ran a hand through his hair and sighed. Feeling homesick—he would not have thought such an emotion possible, but it was clearly present within him.

As was another, perhaps more detrimental—sentiment. Affection.

Not just desire, but actual affection. And for a woman he had sworn to himself he would never touch. A woman that meant a great deal to him and his business.

Sakir closed his eyes and saw Rita beneath him, saw

her eyes flicker with desire one moment, then vulnerability the next, as he took her beaded nipple into his mouth, as he palmed her, as he slid deep within her body.

Sakir groaned, forced his lids to lift, forced his eyes to focus on the black sky littered with stars.

But it helped little.

Her kiss still lingered on his mouth. Her intensity and need. The way she'd exposed herself and her heart to him. The scent of her hair—it intoxicated him even now. And then there was the memory of her eyes as he had pulled her tightly to him...

He wanted more from her, and he would have taken more if his brother's servant hadn't come upon them in the garden.

His body tightened with the urge to run.

He could go to her now...

Just a few floors below, she lay asleep in his bed. Their bed. They were married after all. A legal union that bound them together...

Sakir's chest tightened painfully.

How would she react if he went to her? If he ripped back those silk sheets and lay atop her, his mouth ready to please her however she wished and the lower half of him hard as stone?

Sakir inhaled deeply, calling for calm within his skin, begging for the control he had spent too many years cultivating.

Rita Thompson was his assistant and soon to be his partner. But she would never be his wife. He would do well to remember that. He would also do well to remember that she held the key to his success here in Emand. If things went as planned, she would help him secure one of the largest and most important contracts of his career, while making his brother see what he could do without his family's aid.

This task was of utmost importance.

Sakir straightened. He would remain up here, in the tower, at his desk, at his work.

And Rita would remain in their bed, alone.

Sakir pushed away from the balcony and went inside. For the next three weeks, he would keep his distance, keep his lust in check and hope not to lose his mind in the process.

Eight

Nothing in the world felt better than a great big stretch beneath fine silk sheets in an extra-large bed in a delicious foreign country, Rita thought.

Well, nothing except having the man you'd just been dreaming about in bed with you.

Rita rolled onto her stomach, flipped a wave of tawny hair out of her eye and stared outside at the pink morning. Did the Emand sky always hold such a gorgeous pink hue in the morning? she wondered. And if so, would she be willing to consider transferring her work and her life over here to enjoy it on a daily basis?

Stop.

Rita buried her head in her down pillow and released a little scream. Some amazing kisses, some killer touching, and she was seeing pink skies and imagining a life in Emand. Never mind Sakir's cold impassivity after their encounter. No, she just wanted to remain in the red-hot moment where that beautiful, impassioned man had held her like no other, kissed her breathless and, honest to God, made her bones tingle and shake.

What a fool she was.

A soft knock sounded at her door and for a second Rita felt a flash of excitement in her belly when she thought it might be Sakir. But then a young woman's voice called, "Good morning, Your Highness," and Rita frowned and flipped onto her back.

Gana stood in the doorway. She smiled shyly. "I am sorry to startle, Your Highness."

"That's alright, Gana."

The young maid's smile brightened and she moved into the room with the grace of a ballerina. "Your breakfast is waiting in the living area."

"Thank you." Rita's gaze flicked to the room behind Gana as she asked casually, "Is Sakir— Is… Has my husband been waiting long?"

Gana bit her lip. "His Highness arose very early. He has already taken his meal—"

"Oh?" Why was she surprised? Sure he had to wake up early—didn't want the servants to know he slept on the couch and not in bed with his wife.

Gana continued, "But he has asked me to tell you that he has gone away."

Rita sat bolt upright in bed, her heart in her throat. "What?"

"Just for a few hours, Your Highness," Gana said quickly.

"Oh." With a little laugh of relief, Rita asked, "Do you know where he's gone?"

The young woman shook her head. "I am sorry, Your Highness."

Rita sighed and scooted to the edge of the bed. Obviously, Sakir wasn't all that anxious to see her. Unlike her, he obviously hadn't been that affected by their encounter last night. Or maybe, she mused, with just a little hope left in her heart, maybe he *had* been affected and taking off was his best defense against doing it again when he saw her this morning.

She didn't know whether to be frustrated or flattered.

Well, one thing she wasn't going to be after today was available—sexually, emotionally or otherwise. She'd left herself wide open for hurt last night and had gotten what was coming to her.

No more.

She was through with this fantasy thing. She would uphold her end of the "rules" she'd agreed to with Sakir and try to remember that they'd come here for one reason—business.

"Gana, would you do me a favor?" Rita asked, stepping out of bed and slipping on her robe.

Gana bowed low.

"Would you call me Rita?"

The girl looked horrified. "I could not, ma'am."

"Please. Just when we're alone?"

A smile crept into Gana's face.

"All this formality is getting a little crazy. I need one friend." Rita raised a hopeful brow. "Okay?"

"Okay," she said softly. "Rita."

Rita laughed. "Perfect. Now, let's you and I have a little breakfast together."

Again the young woman looked horrified. "Together?"

"Yep, together." Rita grabbed Gana's hand and led her into the other room. "And if I have to, I'll command it."

As the limousine whisked them into town that afternoon for the welcome feast in the marketplace, Sakir couldn't help but notice the curt set of Rita's mouth as she sat spine-straight on the seat opposite.

She was angry with him.

Even though he knew why she carried such a look of reproach in her blue eyes, the need to change that look to one of heat and pleasure—like the one she'd worn last night—almost corrupted Sakir's sensibilities.

But he knew such a move was unwise. He knew that to touch her again would only lead to both their ruins. He had acted the cool rogue last night to remind them both. They were married but they were not lovers.

Then again, he did care for her. And he was no callous prince. He sat back against the seat, his manner reserved, yet concerned.

"Are you all right, Rita?" he asked.

She stared out the window, into the bright light of day. "Perfect."

"You are cool, distant and professional—it is as though we are at the office."

"Well, we are, aren't we?"

"No, we are not."

She turned, looked at him. "Oh, c'mon. We came here for Emand Oil. That's work in my book."

Sakir glanced at the driver, who was trying to be discreet but could not seem to help looking back at them. Sakir pressed a button on the panel to his left. The privacy glass lifted and set in place. He turned back to Rita. "Yes, we are here to work, but under the guise of marriage."

"Am I not acting enough like a wife, Sakir?" she asked, her tone rich with frustration.

Frustration Sakir also felt, in mind and in body.

His wife…

When they had met in the hall earlier, walked to the car together and took their respective seats inside the limousine, Sakir had made every attempt to keep his gaze from moving over the woman across from him. But at this moment, he felt compelled by some scheming force of nature to take in every inch of her.

Minus the frown, she looked extraordinarily beautiful. She wore a bright blue dress, simple and tasteful, the silk fabric falling softly over her amazing curves. Her hair was pulled back in a pretty bun at her neck, and her skin glowed with health and the fire of a woman whose needs had yet to be met.

His wife.

At that moment, it was a monumental offense that she was not.

He eased out of her complicated question with a comment of his own. "You are angry with me, I know."

She chuckled. "You're quick."

The sarcasm in her voice caused the edges of Sakir's mouth to flicker with amusement. He liked her defiance. He was so accustomed to being catered to and flattered at every turn that he had always appreciated Rita's blunt and spirited attitude. Yes, he liked her fire. Now, if he could only stoke the fire within her in the way he wished.

"You are upset with me for not being at breakfast this morning?" he said. "It could not be helped. I was working and—"

"You are really arrogant, you know that, Sakir?"

"Yes, I do, but to what do you refer?"

She released an irritated sigh. "This isn't about breakfast. This is about last night—"

A rush of need moved through him as he recalled their kiss, her body, his arousal, last night. "Ah, I see."

"No, I don't think you do."

"The kiss, yes?"

"No, Your Highness—the promise."

Sakir paused. "I do not understand, Rita."

She leaned back against the seat, crossed one long, smooth leg over the other. "We agreed to rules. You set them up, Sakir. Don't you remember?"

Of course he remembered. Back in the States when he had honor and a clear head, and no beautiful wife in his bed, he had made those rules.

His jaw tight, Sakir muttered, "I remember."

Tossing her hands up, Rita said, "Then what the hell happened?"

Sakir just stared at her. For the first time in his life, he was without words. Well, not exactly. He had the words, but they were the wrong ones. These words would get him into trouble. How could he explain his actions? Was it wise to admit the truth? That he wanted her and could not control himself? That for the first time in his life he did not want to be in control around a woman—around her? That this is why he had taken her in his arms last night, kissed her like a starving man and forgotten the rules that he himself had set down as law?

She was watching him, her fiery blue eyes digging into his mind, his soul.

He inclined his head. "Again, I apologize for my behavior last night, and for breaking our agreement. It will not happen again."

She shook her head. "That's no explanation, Sakir."

Yes, he knew that. But he also knew that he could not tell her that, just as her mouth had called to him last night, it was actually driving him mad this very minute. He could not tell her that his body craved her almost to the point of pain, that he would bound across the limousine floor, strip her bare and make love to her right now in the light of day if she gave him any sign that she was interested.

Such erotic thoughts had his gut tight and his heart thudding hard and fast against the wall of his chest as the limousine slowed and then stopped.

"We will talk more of this later," he said, forcing back the raging need that was attempting to consume him whole. He gestured to the window. "We are here."

Nine

Rita had loved the Food Network ever since she'd gotten cable one year ago back in Paradise. Friday nights would bring her adventures from Rome, with the best of wine, cheese and pasta, or from Madrid, with seafood paella and Asturian cider, or closer to home, from Chicago, Italian beef sandwiches with all the trimmings.

But her travels only consisted of those through the "boob tube," as her mother had called it, so she'd never felt a part of the experience—never smelled the smells, tasted the wares.

Today, she had stepped into a real live Food Network episode.

Stretched out before her was a glorious marketplace. Under the warm sun and the shade of many vibrant-colored tents, men and women sold fresh vegetables and fruits, breads and succulent meats cooking on spits. They barked at each other, bargained for the best price and then exchanged money and a smile before going on their way.

And in the middle of it all, in the center of so much activity, heat and killer scents, was a decadent red and gold tent with the flag of Emand whipping animatedly at its roof.

"Let us walk," Sakir said from beside her. Then he took her hand and led her from the car into the marketplace.

As they approached, as the royal guards led them closer to the tent, the people stopped what they were doing and looked over at them. For several moments, neither prince nor people said or did anything. Both seemed to be waiting for something to happen. Rita wasn't at all sure what that was. She was about to ask Sakir when he suddenly raised his hand high in the air.

The crowd hushed.

Then Sakir called out to them. Rita didn't understand what he was saying, as it was in Arabic, but it seemed to please the people of Emand very much. When Sakir had finished speaking and his hand had returned to his side, the hands of his people rose to the heavens, followed by joyful shouts and hoots and whirls of sound.

"They welcome us," Sakir said and then turned to Rita. "They welcome you."

Rita glanced up at Sakir. His expression was stately and impassive, but his eyes shone brilliantly. He looked extraordinarily handsome and so princely in his white caftan with gold trim. She wanted to ask him what he was thinking and feeling at that moment as his people cheered him, but she didn't have the chance as he took her hand once again and led her away from the crowd and into the tent.

Once there, Rita's mouth literally dropped open.

She hadn't known what to expect from a welcome-to-the-family type meal from Sakir's people—but certainly not something as lavish and…well, as sensual as what was laid out before her.

Handmade carpets, that in any auction house would surely sell for an astronomical price, covered the floor, their medallion patterns set in bright blues, red and browns, accented with silk. There were pillows strewn everywhere in every color, silk with delicate hand embroidery. To her right stood a buffet-like table of solid gold, laden with trays of food and drink. And in the center of the tent were two sumptuous gold place settings laid out on the carpet floor, with more food and more pillows to lounge upon.

Rita shook her head, awe threading her tone. "They must care for you a great deal to do all of this."

"This has been done for the royal family for centuries," Sakir informed her. "It is a show of respect, that is all."

"Respect. Ah, yes." Rita sat down on the soft rug and eased herself back against one of the pillows. "Hard to believe that anyone could care about you this much, Sakir."

Sakir sat down beside her. "I am not looking for anyone to care for me."

"Are you sure?"

His dark brows lifted. "Where would you get such an idea?"

She shrugged. She wasn't sure herself. Maybe it was that faraway look in his eye when his people had cheered him, or maybe it was this whole mess with Zayad, or maybe it was the way he had looked at her in the limousine when he'd refused to answer her question about last night—with such desire, yet with such conflict. "I suppose I see you differently here. You're not as guarded in Emand as you are in Texas. Your feelings actually rise to the surface once in awhile—" she smiled "—for us common folk to see."

"It is good to see my country and my people." He picked up some flat bread and offered it to her. "As for you being common folk—" his gaze found hers, dark and intense "—make no mistake, you are anything but that, Rita."

A shiver of awareness moved through Rita at his words and at his gaze. "Thank you."

He nodded. "Have some of this." He placed a rich yogurt dish on a plate, followed by a few strips of meat, then handed it to her. "The meat is dried pastrami, aged well. It is delicious."

He was right, of course. Both dishes were wonderful, and Rita ate alongside him very happily. Fried eggplant, pumpkin salad, spicy cheese with tomatoes and onions and a tender lamb shish kebab. Everything was perfectly prepared and seasoned, and soon Rita felt quite satiated.

"I'm surprised we're all alone," Rita said as she relaxed back against her pillow with a cup of Turkish coffee. "That's a first."

"I asked for us to be alone, but if you wish for service it is a simple—"

"No, no." She smiled. "I like this."

He flashed her a devilish grin. "You like that *I* serve you, yes?"

"*Sakir, my humble servant*—yes, I could get used to that."

His eyes darkened as he leaned toward her and whispered, "What may I do for you, Your Highness?"

Rita fairly melted right there. This whole scene was too much. Delicious food, sensual atmosphere. Then there was the man before her, who looked too intense and too sexy, and who was acting as though he would do whatever she asked—no matter how wicked and unwise.

What may I do for you...

Did she dare say, "Kiss me, touch me..."

No. Not after what had happened last night.

When she didn't answer him, Sakir reached behind himself and took a piece of pastry from a nearby tray. "There is another custom that must be adhered to today, in this tent."

Rita's heart fell into her full stomach. "What's that?"

That wicked grin returned. He knew exactly what she had been thinking, imagining...hoping... "It is custom for the husband to feed his wife a piece of baklava at the end of the meal."

She could've slugged him for tormenting her so,

but she fought back with words instead. "Even a royal husband?"

"Especially a royal husband."

"But we aren't 'technically' married. And no one is watching us, so they really wouldn't know if we didn't follow the custom."

Sakir's gaze went dark and reckless. "Perhaps I would like to feed you."

Rita swallowed, her breath a little high in her throat. In the pit of her stomach, a fire raged and the blaze grew more and more out of control with every moment Sakir looked at her that way. How she would quench such an inferno, she did not know, nor did she know how to stop it from snaking lower and lower still down her body.

Sakir held the sweet pastry to her lips. "Would you allow me?"

What else could she do?

She nodded.

"Open your mouth for me," he commanded softly.

With her breath held and her eyelids drifting closed, she did as he asked, hoping to forget all that was behind her and all that remained to be seen and said between them.

She waited, and when he finally placed the delicate pastry in her mouth, time slowed, sweet played her senses and heat rushed her womb.

"Look at me, Rita."

Her lids fluttered open. Her heart thundered in her chest as she looked up into his handsome face. He gazed at her mouth and she silently begged him to kiss her, to run his tongue over her bottom lip and then slip deep into her mouth and make her moan with need.

"How does it taste?" he asked, finding her gaze once again.

"Wonderful. It's wonderful, but…"

"But?"

"I want…"

"More?"

God help her, she nodded again.

Pure desire raged in Sakir's eyes, and Rita felt utterly and gleefully responsible for it. She thought of seizing his face and pulling it toward her, but Sakir was already taking the lead.

He leaned forward, his mouth a whisper away from hers. But it wasn't as she'd hoped. He didn't kiss her. He stayed where he was, so close, not moving, hardly breathing.

Then he turned his head away and cursed darkly in Arabic.

Her body on fire, Rita forced herself to be calm—forced herself to realize the truth. Nothing had changed since last night. This fantasy moment in time that she'd just been imagining—the one with no future and no past—wouldn't give her the kind of pleasure she'd hoped for. Sakir would not allow himself to follow the desire that thundered in his eyes. No. He just sat there, totally in control of his body and his heart, while Rita fought to hold on to the desperate yearning racing through her blood.

"Maybe we should just toss custom right out the window," she began tightly, "and feed ourselves the baklava?"

Sakir nodded, his jaw tight, his lips thin. "Yes, that is one solution."

"You have another?"

Again he cursed and then reached up, touched her face and brushed his thumb over her lower lip. "There is nothing I hate more than leaving you unfulfilled, Rita—" he dropped his hand "—but as you said, we made an agreement. And I must honor it, yes?"

Rita forced herself to nod, feeling rejected, vulnerable and deeply discouraged. She would not fight him, beg him or cajole him into taking what she was so willing to give.

With a sharp exhalation, Rita reached past him, took a slice of the baklava and, this time, fed herself.

"Emand welcomed you and Rita with great enthusiasm today, yes?"

Sakir shut his book with a little too much force and turned to face his brother, who was walking into the palace library where Sakir had been holed up for the last hour with dubious apathy. "They were most gracious."

"They have long awaited your return, Sakir."

"Well, I am afraid they will continue to wait, as I have *not* returned."

Zayad sighed heavily and dropped down into the leather armchair opposite Sakir. "Will you always fight me, brother?"

"I do not know what you mean."

"Yes, you do."

Sakir leaned forward in his chair, his tone tight. "It takes passion to fight. I have none for you."

"No?" Zayad countered, his black eyes filled with indignation.

"No."

"I suppose your only passion is your work, then."

Sakir clipped his brother a nod. "As it will always be."

"That is a lonely business."

Sakir chuckled bitterly. "You lecture me on time spent at my work? What are you but a lonely man of business yourself?"

"I make time for a woman, Sakir."

"Of course. There are many at the sultan's disposal, I know."

Zayad's lips thinned. "I treat all women with respect, and with care." He lifted a brow. "Which is more than I can say for you."

"What the hell does that mean?" Sakir demanded.

"What of your wife?" Zayad leaned back in his chair once more, crossed his arms over his chest.

"What about her?"

"Is she a 'passion,' Sakir?"

Sakir narrowed his eyes. He did not like his brother's presence here, nor did he like this line of questioning. "Rita is none of your affair."

Zayad snorted. "Nor yours, I am told."

Sakir shot to his feet. "I will let you have your library, Your Royal Highness."

Zayad also stood and met his brother eye to eye. "What game do you play, Sakir? You come here with this woman, whom you obviously lust after, and admire as well, I think, but I hear from—"

"Zayad, you would do well to curb your tongue," Sakir warned.

Zayad released a bark of bitter laughter. "You command me?"

"I do." Through gritted teeth, Sakir added, "But I fear not your reprimand. What more can you do to me that has not already been done?"

For a moment, Zayad only stared at his brother, his breath coming tight and clipped. Then he said, "You act as though I banished you from Emand, that I took our parents from us—that I killed Hassan—"

"You did kill Hassan," Sakir uttered darkly.

Zayad turned bloodred. "Our brother's death was an accident."

"An accident he met with because you forced him into the army before he was ready."

"It was his wish!" Zayad bellowed.

"You were the elder brother!" Sakir shouted. "You were to know better."

"What's going on here?"

Both men whirled toward the doorway. Rita stood there, her brow creased. "I could hear you two all the way up the stairs."

Sakir looked away, feeling as though he would explode from the fury in his blood.

"I apologize if we disturbed you, Rita," Zayad said,

his tone princely once again. "We were having a disagreement about the past."

"There is no disagreement about the *truth*," Sakir said. Then he left his brother where he stood, stalked past Rita and left the room.

He heard Rita call after him, "Sakir? Wait, stop." But he kept going, his pace hectic. He was still caught up in that confrontation with his brother—a confrontation that had been a long time coming. Sakir had always thought that saying those words to Zayad would finally release him from the pain of loss.

But he felt only more burdened.

His hands balled into fists.

Rita came running after him. "Where are you going?"

"Out," he barked. "Where I can breathe."

He didn't look back, didn't care if his strides were those of a panther. But Rita kept up somehow. She followed him outside, through the gardens and down a flight of steps. The warmth of the day was starting to fade, but Sakir's blood ran too hot to notice.

When he finally reached the stables, he whipped open one of the stalls and led out one of his brother's large gray stallions.

"Sakir, talk to me."

"Go back to the palace, Rita," he barked, quickly bridling the stallion.

"No. You need a friend right now even though you're too damn stubborn to admit it."

In one swift move, Sakir hoisted himself onto the back of the horse. "You should not be around me right now."

"Why not?"

Damn her. Why could she not just do as he asked for once? "I am in a dangerous mood."

She sniffed. "I'm not afraid of you, Sakir."

"Perhaps you should be."

She ignored him. "Well, I'm going all the same—on your horse or one of my own. And I'm not that good a rider. I have no idea how to put on a saddle, so I'll have to go bareback like you. And I could fall and break a bone or get a concussion or—"

She never finished her sentence as Sakir growled with frustration, grabbed her under the arm, lifted her up and placed her behind him.

"Wrap your arms around me," he ordered.

This time, she did as he commanded. It was a good thing, because when he bellowed at the stallion in Arabic, the animal nearly flew out of the stables, racing toward the desert and the coming sunset.

Ten

The stallion's hooves pounded the sandy floor below as Rita and Sakir rode hard and fast with absolutely no communication. Rita could only guess at how long they'd been gone. A half hour seemed likely, as around them the sun set in a fiery dance of orange, pink and red. It was a jaw-dropping sight, and even though her backside felt bruised from the constant smack against the stallion's spiny back, Rita wouldn't have traded the view for anything in the world.

She'd seen many pictures of the desert of Joona, imagined its snakelike patterns in the sand and wondered if the air would be heavy with heat and spices. But as it was in the marketplace today, the reality was so far from the fantasy it wasn't even funny.

The desert stretched for miles and miles, tawny in color with just a hint of rust thanks to the setting sun beyond. The air, as it brushed her face, was scented, not with spice, as she had imagined, but with the rain that had fallen so light and fresh that morning.

It was like something out of a movie to be riding bareback, behind a handsome sheikh, his white caftan whipping in the wind.

But this was no movie.

There were real feelings here, real emotions at play, and all of it was incredibly complicated. In the marketplace today, Sakir had practically seduced her and then pulled away, angry and unfulfilled—again. Then later, he'd been in one heck of a knock-down, drag-out fight with his brother, whom he then pulled away from, angry and disgruntled.

Rita tightened her hold on his waist.

Would he ever let anyone in? Would he ever let her get close enough to see what pain was in his heart?

The questions in her mind evaporated as Sakir slowed his horse and brought him to a stop. The beast was breathing heavy and glistening with sweat. He snorted and pranced in a circle, then came to a stop once again.

"Where are we?" Rita asked, her throat dry from the sandy wind.

"Mid-desert."

"It's beautiful."

"Yes."

"And peaceful."

Sakir slid easily off the stallion's back. "Thankfully, it is that as well."

"It's so vast. You can't see a thing but sand for miles." She glanced down at him. "Are you sure you know how to get back?"

He offered her his hand. "I would never be lost in the desert."

No, she imagined he wouldn't. Where the heavy traffic of the Texas highways, even the moderate amble of the streets in and around Paradise, might pose a hazard to this man's sense of direction—as he always relied on his chauffeur to get around—he was definitely at home here in this wild vastness.

And for Rita, nothing could be sexier.

Sakir helped her down from the horse, then released her and dropped to the sand. He lay back, looked up at the peach sky.

Rita sat down beside him. "Listen, Sakir—"

"I do not wish to talk."

"I know, but—"

He sighed. "But you will continue anyway."

"I think it's a good idea."

"And force me to speak, yes?"

She didn't bother agreeing. "I heard what you and your brother were saying and—"

"Listening to another's conversation—"

"It's rude and dishonest, I know. I didn't mean to listen." She picked up a handful of warm sand and let it filter through her fingers. "I came to find you and didn't know how to interrupt gracefully."

He put a hand behind his head. "You would do best to forget what you heard."

"From the way you two were arguing I'd say that's easier said than done." Without thinking too much about what she was doing, she lay down beside him and looked up at the same sky. She felt close to him, close enough to ask, "You had another brother?"

Sakir said nothing.

She tread lightly. "You accused Zayad of causing his death?"

He inhaled deeply. "I did."

"Why?"

"Dammit, Rita."

"I know. I'm a pain in the butt. But I think you need to talk about this."

"You think?"

"Yes."

"You are my assistant, not my psychologist."

"Actually here in Emand, I'm your wife," she said with a lightness in her tone. "And I think that entitles me to nudge you a little."

Sakir groaned and cursed again. But to Rita's amazement and satisfaction, he also began talking.

"Hassan, my younger brother, he wanted to follow in our father's footsteps. He had the mind and the heart of a warrior. He wished to enter the army before he was of age. I opposed this, but Zayad allowed him to go." Sakir paused. He seemed to be waiting for someone else to say what came next. But no one did. "Hassan was killed in a foolish training exercise only a few short weeks later. It was a training assault on several abandoned buildings near the east end of town. There were explosions and rifle fire, and the attack caused a nearby building to burst into flames. Hassan perished in the blaze."

Rita turned on her side and faced him, touching his arm. "Oh, Sakir, I'm so sorry."

"I want no pity from you, just as I want no explanations from Zayad."

Rita held fast to his arm. She wasn't put off by his abrasive words. She knew they stemmed from pain. She also knew that it was best for him to get everything off his chest. "Did you leave Emand when Hassan died?"

He nodded brusquely.

"Why?"

"After that, I wanted nothing to do with my family, with Zayad."

Rita watched him, so proud and in such pain, and she wanted to comfort him. But how? This man was such an island unto himself, unapproachable at times. Could she cuddle up next to him? Kiss him? Tell him that she was here for him, if only he'd just accept her?

Slow and easy, she reached out and touched his face. She waited for him to flinch, to turn his head, reject her show of care. But he didn't.

He let her touch him.

Rita smiled. He was so warm, and she reveled in the feel of his strong jaw and the roughness of his day's growth of beard against her skin.

Sakir turned his head toward her, took her hand and kissed her palm. The simple gesture of acceptance and thanks was too much for Rita, and she released a soft sigh of pleasure. She silently prayed he wouldn't stop there, that his mouth would search for hers.

"I have made a promise to you," he whispered, his voice husky and tight.

"I know," she said breathlessly.

"This is the danger I spoke of when you insisted on coming with me."

"I'm not afraid of this happening." Her gaze searched his, the ache in her body loud enough to echo over the miles of the desert. "But you are afraid."

"Rita…"

"Why, Sakir?"

On a growl, Sakir rolled, was poised atop her in seconds. "It is the need I feel for you that I fear." His gaze roamed her face, his eyes forest-green and heavy-lidded. "There is such desperation running through my blood that I fear."

"What are you desperate for?" she asked him, her thighs brushing his as warmth surged into her.

"I have wanted you since the day we met. I want you now."

Rita couldn't believe what she was hearing. Her illusive fantasy was admitting that he wanted her.

Was it the magic of the desert that had spurred this on or pure truth?

Well, she didn't care what it was. She pressed her hips up, felt Sakir hard against her belly. "Take me, then."

He said nothing, but his thigh moved in between her legs.

"Take what you need, Sakir."

"And tomorrow?" he asked, his gaze steady, but passion-filled.

"I won't question tomorrow," she said in all honesty. "We'll leave whatever happens between us right here."

Sakir didn't move for a moment. Then he lowered his face to hers and brushed his lips over hers. "It is impossible."

She wasn't sure what he was referring to. Maybe it was everything. A day making love in the desert was impossible to forget, or trying to stop what was happening between them. She didn't know and didn't care. She said, "Impossible, probably. But inescapable, I think."

"Yes. I agree."

Sakir watched the flush of desire surge into Rita's cheeks. No woman made him feel as this one did, and he imagined no one ever would again. Life was unjust. In all things, he was master. Always controlled, always assured. But in Rita's company, he became a man—just a man—with a lust so reckless he believed he'd be close to death if it were not satisfied.

At this moment, he cared not for promises made and broken.

He wanted her mouth, her tongue, her skin.

His hands went first to her face, then moved to her neck and threaded into her hair. On a soft sigh, she closed her eyes, parted her lips and smiled.

Such perfection made him mad and he covered her mouth with his.

Instantly, her hands wrapped around his neck. Sakir sunk into her warmth and deepened his kiss. She tasted like honey and heat, and he wanted more, more, all she would give him. He changed the direction of his head, slipped his tongue between her lips and met hers with wet, warm passion.

On a groan, Rita thrust her hips up. Sakir answered her call, pressed his thigh up between her legs.

Rita sucked in a breath, her hands raking down, gripping his backside.

Sakir moaned. "You demand and give at the same time."

"To you, I would give anything," she uttered breathlessly.

Her words filled his soul, made him want to rip her clothes from her body and plunge deeply inside her.

But he took his time.

She kissed him with such passion as she gripped his buttocks. "Do you like this, Your Highness?"

"I like it very much, as you most assuredly can tell."

"I wasn't certain," she said coyly.

He took her hand and tunneled it between them, placed it on his shaft. "All you, my love."

He felt her go still beneath him at his words. He was such a damn fool. He had to learn to curb his wicked tongue around her. What had made him speak so?

He knew the answer—the heat, the moment, her long, sensuous body wrapped around him.

He nuzzled her mouth, felt he should explain, say something. "Rita—"

"No, don't." She lifted her chin and lapped at his lower lip with her tongue. "Please."

Sakir felt himself nod. All right. Yes. Forget. It was good for them both.

He sucked her tongue into his mouth, played with it, then kissed her intensely as the sand blew around them and as the sun dipped dangerously into the horizon. It would be twilight soon, but it mattered little to Sakir. He needed to feel Rita, taste her skin.

He eased to the side, took her face with him, his mouth working hers with needful passion. With true access to her now, he moved to the edge of her blouse, slipped his hand beneath and crawled up her hot skin. He felt her shiver and release a whimper into his mouth. The anticipation of cupping her breast and laving her nipple almost caused him to climax right then and there.

But he fought for control.

Up he moved, his fingers inching over her stomach until finally, finally he met with the silky fabric of her bra. With a quick snap, he released her heavenly flesh from its confinement and moved in.

His groin pulsed, seized with need as he cupped her breast. The heavy weight, the hard nipple stabbing into his palm. Madness took him and he ripped away from her mouth, whipped up her blouse and dipped his head.

Paradise was here.

His mouth closed around her nipple with perhaps

too much force. But she didn't cry out in pain. Instead, she took his head and pulled him closer.

Searing heat shot through Sakir and seed leaked from his arousal. With all thought gone, he found the button to her pants and tore, then tugged the flaps apart. He couldn't get to her fast enough—to her heat—to see if she too burned with their shared passion.

And when his fingers finally found her, finally moved through the soft tuft of hair between her legs, pleasure suffused his lungs.

It was as he'd hoped.

She was soaking wet.

Without a word or a sound, he slipped two fingers inside her. He smiled against her breast when he heard her gulp for air, but quickly continued his ministrations to her taut nipple, suckling, nipping.

Around them, the desert warmth started to ease, but between them a fire raged.

Sweat broke out on Sakir's forehead as he worked her body, his fingers plunging deep into her, further, higher, until his knuckles barred the way. Her hips pumped to his rhythm, as inside he felt her core begin to shudder. The walls around his fingers pulsated. Electricity ripped through her into him.

And she cried out into the desert air.

Sun faded, wind whirled around them as the moments passed, as hips slowed, as cries turned to whimpers, then to breathy sighs.

Sakir assumed that Rita would pull away when her body eased, when her body tired, but she did not. She turned to face him and frantically wriggled down his belly. Without a word, she undid his pants and released his erection.

He felt her warm breath and then her hand on him.

She wrapped the base of him in her fist, then began to move in slow, rhythmic strokes. Up, down. Her hand was so tight on him, he nearly passed out. But he kept his sanity.

For he needed it.

As only moments later, she took him into her mouth.

Sakir roared to the heavens in Arabic, asking for control. But no one answered him.

She played him, suckled him, her tongue dancing over the tip of his erection as her free hand cupped him.

An invisible fist slammed into his gut.

He would climax, lose his mind in mere seconds. Lose his control. Panic warred with desire beneath his skin.

He could not believe what he was allowing to happen. No woman had loved him this way in over ten years. It was the ultimate in power, in control. Could he allow the paltry grip he still held on control to be taken from him?

The answer was no.

"No further," he called out, his voice husky, weak, frustrated.

He knew she would be angry with him and totally perplexed, but he could not help that.

Rita released him, sat back, her gaze fixed on him. "Sakir…"

"I did a very selfish thing in marrying you, Rita," he said as he stood up, righted his clothing.

Rita said nothing, but he imagined she agreed with him.

He watched her snap and button her clothes, then scramble to her feet. She didn't look at him.

Sakir breathed in the scent of her. Felt his muscles, his arousal, still desperately hard, stretch and pulse. He gazed heavenward, took a breath. All for the sake of a contract—and the proof to his brother that he was worth something outside the gold gates of Emand—he had married this woman and turned her life upside down, possibly even damaged her heart in the process.

He was selfish.

He was ashamed.

Without further discussion, Sakir lifted Rita up, placed her on his horse and then swung up in front of her.

"I will ask you to hold on to me one last time," he said.

The words held a double meaning, but Sakir brushed them aside as Rita encircled his waist. This time, her grip on him was just enough to keep her safe and held little warmth.

Around him, the desert grew as dark as his soul. But it was a path Sakir knew well and was comfortable taking. He gave the stallion a kick and felt the wind in his face once again.

Women's lib had come to Emand in slow, though deliberate, strides, and Rita was happy to note that the movement hadn't skipped over the aged man sitting before her and Sakir in the grand offices of the Emand Oil Company.

Asad Qahhar, the head of Emand Oil, was definitely old

school in his dress and manner, but he had a warm, welcoming smile as he listened intently to their presentation.

Naturally, Sakir was doing most of the talking. Which might not have been the best idea, as he was slightly off in his pitch, a rarity for him. And although Rita still had a deep anger running through her veins regarding what she'd come to refer to as "his final rejection" last night in the desert, she couldn't help but feel a little sorry for him. She knew how badly he wanted this deal, and to what lengths he had gone—lengths they had both gone to—in order to get those papers signed.

Asad Qahhar placed the prospectus on the table in front of him, leaned back in his chair and addressed Rita. "I am delighted to see that you have traveled with your husband, Your Highness. It was certainly a pleasure to meet you."

"And you, Mr. Qahhar."

"Wife and business associate." Asad grinned widely at Sakir. "You are a lucky man, Your Highness."

"I think so," Sakir said tightly before returning to the business at hand. "You have seen my proposal, what say you, Qahhar?"

Rita tried to not show her frustration. He'd never acted this way. He was always smooth and easy with clients, no rushing to the finish line. Not today. Today, he was blowing this deal with his cold, quick manner. Didn't he realize this was why they'd come here, why they'd gotten married? His business. Emand Oil.

"It looks very good," Asad told him. "My only concern is that you are living in America now."

Sakir snorted arrogantly. "I fly all over the world for my work. I have never had a complaint regarding my performance."

Asad nodded his head sagely. "I am sure that is true, but you must understand my caution."

"Of course."

"I would like time to think, yes? We will meet again in, say, a week?"

"One week," Sakir repeated, his lips a little thin.

Rita mentally shook her head. The man wanted to think about things over the next week. This wasn't good.

Asad stood, shook Sakir's hand, then bowed to Rita. "Once again, it was a pleasure, Your Highness."

Rita gave him her most brilliant smile, not that she expected that to change the man's mind, but a warm gesture couldn't hurt after Sakir's coldness. "It was wonderful to meet you, too, Mr. Qahhar. Let's hope it's the first of many meetings."

The man returned her smile. "I must come to America soon. I like her people very much."

Rita didn't know what hit her at that moment, but she couldn't stop herself. After all she and Sakir had been through in the last several days, she wasn't about to let him lose this deal and let all her heartache be for not. "Mr. Qahhar, America is wonderful," she began, "but Emand is where true beauty lies. My husband and I plan on spending a good deal of time here."

Asad turned to Sakir, a look of fresh interest crossing his face. "Is that so? Why did you not say as much before?"

Sakir felt as though he'd been punched in the gut. What the hell had made Rita say such a thing? He whirled to face her, but she was avoiding his gaze. Qahhar on the other hand, was not.

"Well, this changes matters, Your Highness," he said. "I will see you both in a week."

Sakir inclined his head. And with a low bow, Qahhar left the room.

Sakir turned to Rita, his tone sharp. "What did you do?"

"We were losing him."

"We were not." Sakir snatched up his briefcase.

"I don't know what's going on with you, if it's about last night or this war with your brother, but you were totally off today and if I hadn't said what I said, this deal would be in the toilet."

Sakir didn't want to hear her explanations. True or false. He only wanted to bark. "'Spending much time in Emand.' I would not consider this, Rita, no matter how much I want the account." He raised a fierce brow at her. "I will have to restate this when Qahhar and I meet again."

"You mean when *we* meet with him again," she corrected.

"I am not certain. Not after what you have done."

She lifted her chin, looking so proud, so determined and so beautiful in her dove-gray suit and flawless complexion. "Oh, I'll be there, Sakir, you can bet your title on it."

Black rage threatened to drown him. He wanted to punch the wall, duel his brother, tell Qahhar to take his contracts and burn them—but most of all he wanted to haul this woman against him and make her body scream with pleasure. If he would allow himself, he would take her in Qahhar's office this very moment.

But he would not.

He had spent the majority of last night on the couch, reminding himself that with her, around her, in her, he was no longer in control.

"So, what's next on the business agenda?" she asked him, her tone flat, all business.

"I have work to finish back at the palace."

She nodded. "Do you need me?"

Fire fisted around Sakir's groin. Damn her. But looking into her impassive blue gaze, he saw that her query was not double-sided.

"I think not."

Again Rita nodded stiffly, slipped her purse under her arm. "Shall we go, then?"

Sakir walked with her out the door and into the halls of Emand Oil. Living life alone was what he had chosen long ago, and it had served him well. This life left no scars, no regrets.

It was safe.

The woman beside him threatened that strange sense of peace. She made him wonder what could be if he chose something different—a fact that made her even more dangerous than he had once thought.

Gana stood beside Rita as she packed some clothes, shoes and personal effects in her overnight case. "This is not wise, Your Highness."

"Relax, Gana," Rita said, her face set with determination, her body rigid with purpose. "I've hired two guides for this journey. A husband-and-wife team, no less. I'll be safe and sound and—" she gave a flash of brittle laughter "—maybe I'll get a little perspective in the process."

Clearly not able to appreciate the beauty of a "little perspective," when a woman was frustrated by her husband, Gana clasped her hands together and sighed. "The sheikh will not approve."

Rita grabbed her bag and headed for the door. "Right now, I couldn't give a damn what the sheikh thinks. I need some alone time."

Without further discussion, Rita left the room. But duty still called Gana, and she would not be so easily lost. She followed Rita down the hall and stairs, out the front door of the palace and into the bright morning sunshine.

"Your Highness," she called. "Rita?"

This made Rita stop and turn around. "What is it, Gana?"

"What is this alone time?" she asked, a little breathlessly from her dash to keep up.

Rita gave a wave to the older man and woman in the Jeep at the far end of the driveway, the couple that knew her as just a visitor, not as a princess, and then said to the sweet little maid, "It's what every woman who's been dumped by a man must take to regain her sanity." She gave her a rueful smile. "Bye, Gana."

"What shall I tell His Royal Highness?" Gana called after her.

With her hand on the door of the Jeep, Rita paused. Then, with a grin, she called back, "Tell him I'll see him in a few days."

The words felt good. As did the open-air Jeep. She was off, headed for the adventure of a lifetime. She'd been wasting time, energy and tears in this place. No more, she thought as they hit the beginnings of the desert.

Caramel-colored sand carpeted the Jeep's way and the hotel-like sounds of the palace gave way to peaceful nothingness, barring the wind and lazy hum of the motor.

All those lovely oases in the desert—the ones she'd read about on the plane ride over—would be part of her experience over the next several days.

And Sakir—well, he didn't need her around, did he? Not until the next meeting with Qahhar, at any rate. And even at that, he'd acted as though she could be miles away and it wouldn't matter.

Well, he was about to get his wish.

Rita sat back, closed her eyes and smiled. A little adventure, no, a lot of adventure, was just what she needed and deserved.

Rita woke with a start. She knew she must have dozed off for a while because the sun was overhead in the sky, and the peaceful sounds of wind and motor had been replaced by a loud whirring sound of a plane.

"We have to stop, Your Highness," her female guide said as her husband brought the Jeep to a sand-skipping halt.

"Why?" Rita asked, still a little lost in sleep.

"Sheikh Al-Nayhal comes."

"What?"

Her heart in her throat, Rita glanced out the window. She saw no other vehicles, no horse and no rider. Above her, the loud whir of the airplane intensified. She looked up. It wasn't an airplane in the sky. A white helicopter fairly floated above them—and it was descending.

Rita watched openmouthed as the enormous machine came to land directly in front of them. The inside of the Jeep felt like a wind tunnel as the blades of the copter still swung. Two seconds later, the door opened and Sakir jumped out.

He wore a dangerous frown as he approached. "Have you gone insane?" he shouted through her window, the noise of motor and wind almost deafening.

"No, I don't think so," Rita shouted back.

"You have run away from the palace, Rita. This is not done."

"Don't tell me what to do, Sakir."

His jaw went rigid.

"And by the way, you're the one who's always running away." She didn't stop, couldn't—even when he gritted his teeth. "Today, it's my turn."

"You will go no further."

"I am not your prisoner, Sakir."

He swung the car door wide. "You are my wife."

She snorted. "Do you really want to go there?"

In the front seat, her two guides were desperately trying to fade into their leather bucket seats.

"I need a break, Sakir," Rita began, her tone serious. "Part of this whole…adventure was seeing and exploring, and I plan on doing both."

He turned away, looking as though he was trying to gather patience or cursing or something equally mannish. "You will continue to fight me on this?" he asked.

"Hard to handle, remember." She cocked her chin. "I did warn you."

He shut the back door, then walked around to the driver's side and said something to her guides in Arabic. Rita's guides nodded and then quickly got out of the car.

"Hey," Rita began.

Without a word to Rita, Sakir shouted something to the helicopter pilot. The man also nodded and then beckoned the tour guides toward the chopper. Rita watched in frustrated anger as the husband and wife climbed into the white machine and closed the door. In seconds, the helicopter was off the ground and flying away.

Sakir walked back around to her door, opened it and said in all politeness, "Please sit in the front with me."

Rita blinked, didn't move. "What the hell did you just do?"

"I will answer you as soon as you change seats."

Rita practically growled as she did as he commanded—slamming doors, dropping into her seat, crossing her arms over her chest.

When Sakir was in the driver's seat, his hand clutching the gearshift, he said, "If you are determined to do this, I will be your tour guide."

"I've already had that kind of adventure," she said, her tone flat. "And you know what?"

He glanced over at her. "What?"

"It wasn't nearly as fulfilling as I'd hoped."

His eyes flashed green fire and he gunned the engine. "What you had, Rita Al-Nayhal, was a taste—just a taste." Then he shoved the gearshift into first and took off.

Eleven

Desert turned slowly into mountain, just as an hour's worth of stubborn silence inside the Jeep turned to frustration. Finally, Rita gave in and spoke. "I believe this is kidnapping."

Sakir glanced over at her, gave her a derisive smirk. "You make a joke, yes?"

"Hardly." She straightened her spine. "I was going along fine, minding my own business, having a nice little adventure, and then you show up—helicopter in tow—and sweep me away."

"Sweep you off your feet, you mean."

"No, that's not what I mean."

"Rita," he said with that patient tone she knew so well. It was the same tone he reserved for impatient clients. "It is a dangerous endeavor what you have tried to do."

"Why?"

"You must understand something. You are royalty now. My wife could be a target to many—"

She snorted. "Your wife."

"That is correct," he said firmly.

Her gaze moved over him. His long, hard body was decked out in a simple pair of tan pants and a white linen shirt. His handsome face was so stubborn; his eyes, gorgeous and intense.

Sigh.

His wife. If that were only true. If only he could stop acting like such an idiot and let that be true. But it wasn't and he wouldn't, so she was no wife—just a business partner. A business partner who was growing tired of all the games being played between them.

She shifted her gaze to the window and the view of the rugged mountains. "So, where are we going?"

"Lake Shami," he said, thrusting the car into second gear as they drove up a steep hillside. "Then we will travel just above it to the palm tree forest."

Rita snapped to attention, forgetting their troubles for a moment to concentrate on something far more intriguing. "Palm tree forest? That wasn't on the tourist maps. I've never heard of such a thing."

"No, you would not. The forest is a very special place, revered and cared for by my people…" He paused, his jaw tightening. Then he released a weighty sigh.

"What's wrong?" Rita asked.

"It is nothing."

Rita replayed the last thing he'd said, then smiled sadly. The "nothing" he didn't want to talk about was obvious to her. "You don't have to be embarrassed for calling them 'your people.'"

"I do not feel embarrassment," he said quickly.

He was so stubborn, so proud. "I'm just saying that for you to feel warmth and show you care for the people of Emand is normal."

"Look ahead, Rita."

Confusion hit her. "What?"

Sakir pointed. "Lake Shami is just over that rise—"

Rita shifted in her seat to face him. "Why is it so hard for men to communicate their feelings?"

"Why must women force these feelings from a man?" he countered.

She shook her head. "You're answering a question with a question."

"My point is thus," he said with deep sincerity. "Why can a woman not be patient?"

At that, Rita paused. She'd never heard him say such a thing. He'd barked, bitten, commanded, but never asked something with vulnerability attached. And she found that the anger in her heart melted a touch.

She took a deep breath. He made a valid point. Had she been pushing him? Not just about releasing his desire for her, but about his feelings regarding Emand, his life here, his relationship with Zayad and his grief over his younger brother?

Perhaps, she thought. Maybe it would be easier and

less stressful for everyone if she just let things happen or not happen, let Sakir make a move, or not, let Sakir confide in her…or not.

"Patience, huh?" She shrugged. "Okay."

Sakir glanced over at her, his brow lifted. "Okay?"

"Yes."

"As simple as that?"

She broke out into a broad smile. "Yes. Now, tell me more about these palm trees."

"See them for yourself." Sakir gestured out the front window.

There it was. Beyond the thick pane of glass. Utter magnificence. Rita could barely breathe as she stared at the sight in front of her. Hundreds of massive, waxy-leafed palm trees grew out of a glorious hillside like an earthy chessboard. And just beyond sat a beautiful and highly inviting lake in the shape of an eight.

"Look there," Sakir said, pointing to a rock wall above the right side of the lake where rain seemed to trickle down.

"Waterfalls?" she asked, excited.

"Yes. One of many."

Reverent silence took them both as they drove down the hillside, between the ancient palms to a vacant stretch of land where Sakir parked the car.

Rita got out of the Jeep first, stretching as hot, wet air enveloped her. She walked a few feet to a small clearing and then looked up. Palm tree leaves framed a patch of blue sky. "This is amazing."

"You know," Sakir said, coming to stand beside her, "you would not have seen it with the guides."

"I know."

"You thank me for coming to get you?"

She laughed. "Let's not get crazy here."

He laughed with her, his eyes crinkling. "Would you care to see the lake? Perhaps take a bit of lunch at the water's edge."

"Lunch?"

He held up a leather satchel.

"But how?"

He grinned wickedly. "I am a man of surprises."

Even in the supreme heat, a shiver of awareness moved through Rita. "Is that so?"

"Yes." He reached out and gently took her hand. "Are you ready?"

She smiled, nodded. "Lead on."

"Ah… So, I am a suitable tour guide, then?"

"Not bad." Her grin widened. "We'll have to see how the day goes."

"That sounds fair," Sakir said. He led her down a makeshift path of sand and rock and palm tree branches to the edge of the lake, and just adjacent to one of the lovely waterfalls. There, he delved into the satchel that she assumed was her tour guide's and came out with a blue and red carpet. He rolled the lovely rug out on a patch of sand, several feet from where the water lapped elegantly at the rocks.

"A carpet…" she began, playing along. "What else have you got in there?"

He raised a brow at her, then proceeded to take out several pieces of flatbread, some delicious-smelling meat and what looked like a cucumber salad.

"Dried lamb," he said, presenting her with his wares just a little bit dramatically. "Olive salad with cucumber and tomato, bread and some cold wine. A meal fit for a princess, I think."

Rita beamed. She couldn't help it. "It's perfect," she said. The whole thing, she mused. The meal, the view, the man—oh, and the possibilities.

No.

She couldn't go there. Wouldn't go there. Whatever happened, if it happened at all, it would come from Sakir and with absolutely no pressure *for* her.

Under the shade of a massive palm tree, they ate their lamb, bread and salad, drank their sweet, cold wine, then promptly relaxed back on the soft carpet and enjoyed the view.

"I love the water," she said, sipping her wine. "Comes from being a Pisces I guess."

"What is this Pisces?"

"It's an astrological sign for those born in March and the symbol is a fish."

He nodded. "Yes, I see now. I am August first. What does this make me?"

Rita started laughing.

"What?"

"You're a Leo, Sakir."

He raised his brow, clearly not understanding.

"The lion," she prompted.

An arrogant grin broke on his face. "Lion. I like that."

"I thought you might," she said drily.

"Lions love the desert as fish love the sea."

She nodded. "Although lakes are my favorite. They're so calm, so peaceful." She took another sip of wine. "Do you know if this one is spring-fed?"

"I think it is. And reported to be rather cool in temperature." He cocked his head, grinned. "But welcome on such a hot day, yes?"

His black hair was damp with sweat at the temples and nape. He looked sexy and full of sin, and, God help her, she was ready to ask him to kiss her.

How could one man make her so weak? She had her principles, she had a code of honor among women—the code that clearly stated, "I will not beg for sex." But around Sakir, when he looked at her with those dark eyes and come-hither mouth, she was lost.

"We could take a swim if you wish," he said.

A flush of excitement warmed her cheeks. "You're not restricted to waiting one hour?"

"What?"

"In America, there is sort of a waiting period after eating."

"Interesting." He grinned. "I suppose I like to live dangerously."

"Do you really?" she asked, unspoken questions threading her tone.

Sakir stood, seeming as tall and imposing as the palms around him. "I suppose I would not be a proper tour guide if I did not accompany you into the water."

Rita swallowed thickly, the heat in her belly pulsating, then dipping low. "I think it's only right."

Before Rita had time to think, Sakir was unbuttoning his shirt. With greedy eyes, she watched him as he so casually removed the pressed linen. Her hands itched to touch him, run her fingers down his chest, her nails over his washboard stomach. His bronzed chest was smooth and thick with muscle and she thought she'd never want to look at anything else ever again.

Until her gaze slipped a few inches.

Her breath caught in her throat, and the muscles in her womb contracted.

His pants lay a foot away, and he wore no underwear. He was glorious. Long, lean and hard from head to foot.

"So, you're going skinny-dipping, huh?" she asked weakly, lust running rampant through her body.

"Did you have another suggestion?"

She shook her head. "No, you look amaz—" She shut her mouth, took a breath and began again. "What I mean to say is, I was going to wear my bra and panties. It's sort of bathing suit-like and—"

"What happened to living dangerously?" he asked.

"That was you."

A grin flickered at the corner of his mouth. "No, Rita. That is you as well. For as long as I've known you."

She didn't know how to respond to such a statement. If she looked back at her life since knowing Sakir, she wouldn't call herself bold or dangerous. Well, not in romance anyway. In business, perhaps. And then there was her fantasy life…

Okay, there she was bold. There she lived dangerously.

"You disappoint me," Sakir said, a thread of boyish discontent in his tone.

Rita rolled her eyes. "Well, I would hate to do that."

"You have a beautiful body, Rita. There should be no shame in revealing it."

Her cheeks burned and she tried not to stare at his burgeoning arousal. "There is definitely shame when you have big thighs and a bigger butt." She shrugged. "I keep meaning to join a gym, but—"

"Take off your clothes."

She looked up at him through her lashes. "Are you commanding me again?"

"Yes. Do as I say."

Rita inhaled deeply. She knew Sakir was only half-serious in his order, that he was being playful in such a sensual setting. And God help her, she wanted to play along with him. After all, she'd decided only an hour ago to leave the decisions and the come-ons to Sakir.

She'd decided this and yet she felt so odd, so vulnerable suddenly. He stood before her, totally at ease—barring nine and half inches of arousal.

If only she could be so calm.

Slowly, and very unsurely, she stood up and began to peel off her clothes from her hot, sticky skin one piece at a time.

She felt Sakir's gaze on her and wanted to run behind a palm, but she held her ground. Finally, she stood before him in her bra and panties.

Sakir shook his head, grinned with sinful intent. "You are not finished."

Rita's breasts tightened, tingled, begged for release, perhaps for this man's hands. She made a futile groaning noise, then said, "Fine."

First, she removed her bra and sighed as warm air moved over her jutting nipples. Then she slipped her fingers under the band of her panties and eased them down.

She stood before him nude, feeling his stare, feeling embarrassed and totally vulnerable.

Sakir walked to her, his hand slipping around her waist. "You make me weak with need, Rita. Feel how weak." He eased her close, and she felt him hard against her belly. "You are so beautiful, perfect, with a woman's curves."

Rita shut her eyes, her legs weak as water, her mind filled with chaotic thoughts and visions of making love to this man in the lake beyond, under the waterfall.

Sakir touched her chin, lifted her eyes to his. "Let us enjoy the water."

She smiled, wondering idiotically if he'd heard her thoughts as the heat rose and suffused them, and as Sakir led her into the cool water.

The sand yielded to her steps as they waded deeper and deeper, until the water was up to their shoulders.

"This feels too good," she said.

"I know," he said, wrapping his arms around her and pulling her close.

This time there was no discussion of what was right or wrong. His mouth collided with hers, his tongue dipping into her mouth, searching for her. Rita sucked in a breath, wrapped her arms about his neck and deepened her kiss.

"I am a weak man," Sakir uttered.

"And I am glad for it," she whispered.

His hands raked down her back, squeezing her buttocks, the pads of his fingers digging into her flesh. Rita trembled furiously, but thanks to the buoyancy of the water, she managed to wrap her legs around his waist.

His mouth slipped from hers and went to her ear. "I will bring you such pleasure, Rita."

"But will you ever take pleasure?" she asked, her voice hoarse.

He thrust two fingers inside her, silenced her. "Watching you *is* my pleasure."

Rita gasped for breath, the sensation of liquid fire hugging stiff fingers that bucked up against her womb so wonderful she thought she'd collapse or slip beneath the water and drown.

But she was meant to live, meant to ride his fingers, cry out as he used his thumb, rough and experienced on the bundle of nerves at her core.

His mouth moved to her neck, his teeth grazing her flesh as her heart pounded a rhythm of sex. Water splashed around them, and despite its coolness, sweat broke out on Rita's forehead. Climax was imminent. Her legs shook, her breath was coming in short, raspy waves.

Sakir pulled out his two fingers, then plunged three deeply inside her. Rita opened her mouth in a silent scream of pleasure. Her release was so close, as Sakir flicked her between his thumb and forefinger.

Suddenly she tensed, her body shaking, her mind blank, and let the rush of orgasm pound her senses.

Then all she felt was water and air. She sagged against Sakir, her breath coming in gasps. He rubbed her back and whispered soothing words in Arabic in her ear. She wished with all her heart that she could have this moment forever.

But then the fantasy turned to reality again, just as the fine weather turned to gray.

Sakir kissed her mouth, both with gentleness and with desire. "The clouds move in. Rain is coming."

"We haven't finished this."

"No, we have not."

Hope surged into her heart. "Really?"

"Back at the palace, in our bedroom, we will start this and we will finish it." He lifted her in his arms and started back to shore. "But we must go now."

"I don't want to," she said, turning into his chest, his warmth, knowing she sounded like a child, but not particularly caring.

When Sakir reached the sand, he set her down with supreme gentleness and said, "Nor I," then began to help her on with her clothing.

Midnight.

Sakir stared at the moon.

Midnight, and he still hadn't gone to the rooms he shared with his "wife."

When he and Rita had returned to the palace, the sky had been dark and she had just been waking from a nap in the Jeep. Sakir's immediate thought had been to take her upstairs and make love to her in their bed. He was ready, in mind and most assuredly in body. But something had kept him from that wondrous task.

Perhaps it was his spirit.

With a tone of regret, he'd told Rita that he had several phone calls to return and he would see her later. She gave him no fight, as no doubt she was growing used to his change in mood and in mind. A fact that shamed Sakir to his very bones. Though he gave himself to no one and gave pleasure whenever he was given pleasure, he had always remained a forthright and honorable man when it came to women.

The problem was Rita.

She was not just any woman.

She was fire and life, and he was growing too close to her. Wanting her too much. And, most troublesome of all, needing her too much.

Sakir walked further into the garden and let the scents of jasmine assault his muddled senses. He passed the sculpture of his grandfather, bronzed and ominous. He passed the walled rock garden and mint bushes. He passed the koi pond, knowing exactly where he was going and refusing to stop.

Finally he did.

The stone erupted from the ground before him.

Exotic plants Sakir himself had chosen surrounded his brother's grave. In the daytime, the plants attracted a variety of butterflies, for Hassan had loved butterflies as a child. At night, there was only a lush stillness to the spot.

Sakir stood there for a long time, meditating on all the years lost to his brother. Anger pulsed in his blood.

What a waste.

"Sakir?"

He didn't turn around. The voice acted like a balm to his anger. Rita. He felt her come up beside him, then watched from the corner of his eye as she knelt down and brushed her fingers over the words he'd had carved into the stone.

"What does this mean?" she asked.

His throat tight, Sakir uttered, "'Your brother misses you, little one.'"

Rita stood, then did the strangest thing. She took his hand and held it in her own. She felt warm and real and he wanted to pull her close and gather her up in his arms.

But he did not.

"How did you find me?" he asked.

"You like this garden."

"It is late."

"I know."

"You should be in bed."

She squeezed his hand. "So should you."

He sniffed. "Sleep has eluded me for ten years."

"Who said anything about sleep?"

Sakir turned. She stared up at him, her gaze soft and tender. On any other night, any other day, Sakir would have worried at such a look. But not tonight, not with her. He needed her warmth and care, and was ready to take it.

His gaze flickered down her body. She wore a pale

blue silk nightgown that molded to her curves and she carried the matching robe in her hand.

"I chose that gown for you," he said, desire cleaving to every muscle, every bone.

She smiled. "I know."

"You are breathtaking, Rita."

Her smile widened. "Let's go to bed, Sakir."

He nodded, then slipped his hands underneath her and lifted her into his arms. When she raised a brow at him, he said, "It is tradition."

"What is, exactly?" she asked as he walked through the garden.

Sakir said nothing until they were up the palace stairs and standing before their bedroom door. Once there, he leaned in and kissed her softly. "It is tradition for the prince to carry his princess over the threshold on their wedding night."

Rita laughed softly. "A little past that, aren't we?"

Sakir opened the door and headed for the bedroom. "We have never made love, Rita." With great care, he placed her down on the bed. "We had no wedding night." With slow, tender fingers he eased her nightgown up, up over her knees, up past her thighs. "I think this will be our wedding night, yes?"

Rita felt as though she were dreaming. Sakir talking of wedding nights as he removed her nightgown, her lace panties and his own white caftan. Sakir standing above her, totally nude, his body tight, his erection thick and ready.

Yes, this had to be a dream.

Sakir gazed down at her. "I wish to give you pleasure first, but I do not think I can—"

"Sakir I want you inside me," Rita said, her arms reaching for him. "You have no idea how much pleasure that will give me."

He released a weighty breath. "I want to tease you, taste you, feast between your—"

"I have been teased long enough."

A slow grin moved over Sakir's face. "Yes. We both have."

Rita watched as he quickly sheathed himself. Her breath held tight with anticipation, she waited. What would he feel like? Would she stretch enough to accommodate him? Would she please him? Would she make his climax as intense as he'd made hers?

Sakir moved above her. His gaze fixed on hers, he spread her thighs apart with gentle insistence. Then he lowered his hips.

Rita felt him, up against the entrance to her body. Just from the anticipation alone, she was very wet. Sakir moved up and down, teasing her as he watched her. But that's as far as he went. Never in her life had Rita been so excited, so curious.

His face so near hers, his breath so close, she asked, "What's wrong?"

He shook his head. "I do not know. This seems sacred somehow. I have never known such intensity of feeling."

Rita's heart thundered in her chest. She had known

nothing like this, either. But she did know how to name it. She was in love with her husband and no words, no reason, could keep her from it.

She wrapped her legs around his waist, urging him down, inside, deep into the wet heat of her body.

On an oath, Sakir slipped his hand underneath her hips, lifted her up and pushed into her.

"Yes," Rita uttered, tilting her hips up further as she reveled in every slow inch he gave her.

He was hers.

For now.

For this wonderfully delicious moment.

"Move with me," he said, as his slow strokes quickened.

"Yes." She slammed her hips to meet him, following him to that fast and frantic pace that knew no end but orgasm.

She just wanted to release, wanted to remove all thoughts of the past and how she and Sakir had gotten to this point. She just wanted now. Over and over again, if he'd oblige her.

Her muscles tightened around his shaft as Sakir drove into her. Sweat trickled down her back. Her breasts rose and fell. Time evaporated.

"When you climax," Sakir said through fraught breaths. "I want to hear you. Scream, cry, call out to the gods. Whatever is in you. But I must hear it. Do you understand?"

She nodded violently. Yes. She understood him. She would not hold back. Lord, anything he asked of her she would do. And his request was timely. The love in her heart was ready to explode; the volcano bubbling inside her was ready to flow, rip a hole in her heart, make her see stars.

And when Sakir lowered his head and took her nipple between his teeth as he drove into her hard and fast, she did just that.

Explode. Come.

Die. Live.

"Come with me now," she cried out, gripping his back with her fingers, her nails, she wasn't sure.

Sakir pounded into her. Over and over. His breathing rapid, his body wet with sweat.

Rita let her head fall back. Deep in her throat a cry erupted as torrents of fire, rain and electric shock rippled through her.

And Sakir went with her, uttering her name a thousand times as he spilled hot seed deep into her core.

Twelve

Sakir watched the pale pink light of sunrise play over Rita's nude body, just barely covered by the blue silk sheet from their bed. Up he roamed, his gaze moving from ankle to knee, to hip, to belly, to full breast and supple nipple.

Glorious.

He shuddered and rolled to his back.

What had he done? What had he allowed to happen in this bed? Had his lack of control and propriety disintegrated under the burning light of desire?

And did he care?

The answer to the final question was spirited away as Rita shifted beside him. The tangled silk sheet covered only her woman's curls, leaving the full view of her chest and belly to his roguish eyes. No, he did not care for control or propriety. He wanted to wake this sleeping beauty with a kiss on first one set of lips, then the other.

He felt himself grow hard at the thought. He turned to his side, faced her.

Again, she shifted. This time she rolled to him, snuggled into his chest. Her mouth moved over his skin, and her throaty whisper clawed at his groin. "You're up early?"

"You are very observant."

She laughed, her warm breath fanning against his chest. "You know what I mean."

"I sleep little."

"You told me." She nuzzled her nose against his nipple. "A lot on your mind?"

She would never know how much… "Yes."

Rita glanced up. "But I must be patient and not ask, right?"

Her wide blue eyes fairly drew him in, deep into pools of an understanding heart. He wanted to jump most sincerely. Get lost—or found.

He fairly sighed. Never had he expressed what lay weighty on his heart. Never had he wanted to. But the burden was growing heavier as of late. Rita had offered him her ears too many times to name; as he looked into her blue eyes, he saw empathy.

The words slipped from his lips far too easily. "With so much death and destruction in my family, I fear I am dead inside."

Yes, far too easily. His gut clenched with shame and he wished for the words back. But Rita was already set on her task. She wrapped her arms around his neck, her leg around his groin and pulled herself to him.

"I can assure you, you're very much alive."

Sakir's chest constricted with a tenderness he'd never had before today. He ran his hands down her back to her buttocks and pulled her closer.

Rita searched his gaze. "Tell me what you're thinking."

"I wonder if I am capable of loving. I wonder if I will ever allow myself to fly free." He wanted to look away as shame gripped him. Men of his rank did not say such things. In fact, they should not even feel such things. "I wonder if I will ever feel trust for anyone again."

"Sakir…"

He shook his head. "I do not say this for answers or for your pity, Rita."

"I know that."

"I tell you this because I care for you and want you to understand who I am and what I cannot give."

He saw her once steady gaze flicker, but she said firmly, "I've never asked for anything."

"No, but you deserve all."

A sad smile touched her beautiful mouth. "I don't want to talk about this anymore."

"You wished for me to tell you my feelings, yes?"

"Yeah, I did, but not now—not here, not today." She pressed her hips to him tentatively. "We have almost a week of fantasy left before reality sets in."

Sakir released a bitter chuckle. He understood only too well the need to suspend reality for as long as possible. Had he not attempted such a feat with this unsound romance several times before?

They had two weeks before they returned to the States, and to something resembling reality. Soon enough, he would have to face all those fears, those devices of protection, he had shared with Rita and decide once and for all if he could release his death grip on them.

"You wish for fantasy?" he asked, a slow grin cutting across his mouth.

Rita smiled and nodded enthusiastically.

"Done." Sakir rolled to his back, lifted Rita up over him and then slowly eased her down on his hard shaft.

She let out a joyful moan and white-hot pleasure ripped into Sakir. The wet glove of her body seemed to suckle his erection as she began to move, as she ground her hips against him.

Back and forth.

Deeper.

She grabbed his hands, thrust them to her breasts. She arched her back, let her head drop. And she rode him. Hard and intense.

Sakir couldn't take his eyes off of her as she slammed her hips against him, thrusting, going wild, her breasts quivering with the movement.

But the sight was too much for him to bear and he closed his eyes, let his mind run blank, let his body sink into the oblivion of pleasure.

Rita watched him as he ate his lunch, so perfect, so refined in his manner. She hid behind a potted plant and wondered if she should approach him as he sat before the grand marble table in the most exquisite of atriums. Granted, she wasn't a meek little mouse. But the guy was a sultan, for goodness sake. Pretty intimidating for a girl from a small ranching town in Texas.

Then again, she wasn't the intimidated type.

Rita took a deep breath, stepped out from her leafy cover and started toward him. But she only made it about five feet before she was grabbed from behind and hauled forward.

Panic jumped in her blood as she struggled against decidedly Neanderthal-like muscles. "Hey. Let me go! What's the big idea?"

Without explanation, she was dragged forward. Her heart was in her throat; she wondered what was about to happen to her. What kind of punishment she would receive for approaching the Sultan of Emand unannounced?

"Your Royal Highness." The very low, masculine voice came from just behind her left ear, from the Neanderthal. "This woman has been watching you."

Zayad Al-Nayhal turned casually and gave Rita an inquisitive smile. "Is this true, Rita?"

"Can this guy let me go, please?" Rita said tightly.

"Of course." Zayad motioned to the man behind her. "The princess wishes to be released."

"Princess…" The man sputtered, then quickly stepped back.

"And for the record, I wasn't watching you." Rita

sniffed proudly. "I was waiting for you to finish your lunch before I came to talk to you, that's all."

Zayad nodded at his servant. "You may go now, Laul."

Rita glanced back just in time to catch a glimpse of her captor. Big, brawny and totally bold, Laul bowed low, then turned and left the room.

"I apologize for my servant's brutish behavior." Zayad lowered his head a fraction. "But one cannot be too careful."

"When one is in power, is that it?"

Zayad smiled. "You understand." He motioned to the chair beside him. "Would you care to join me?"

She arched a brow. "Will I have to be strip-searched beforehand?"

His grin widened. "I will leave such a pleasure to my brother."

Heat shot into Rita's cheeks.

Zayad chuckled. "Please sit down. What can I do for you?"

Struggling to gain her composure, Rita took a deep breath and dropped into the chair beside him. "I want to talk about you and Sakir."

The smile fell away from the sultan's face. "As you have seen and no doubt heard, there is no love lost between brothers." His gaze clouded with pain, but remained steadfast on hers. "He believes me responsible for our brother's death and will not hear my opinion on the matter."

"I know. He told me."

"So if you do not come for answers, what do you come for?"

"The thing is, Your Highness, I believe that the circumstance surrounding Hassan's death isn't the real reason for Sakir's antagonism."

Zayad looked startled, though intrigued. "No?"

She shook her head. "I think he's scared."

Zayad snorted and puffed up his chest. "The men of my family do not feel fear, my sister."

Rita rolled her eyes. "Well, that's ridiculous."

Zayad's black eyes hardened, and for the first time since she'd met him, Rita felt very small and very insignificant. But she forced herself to remain calm and focused. She was here to make Zayad understand where his brother was coming from, because the spirit of the man she was in love with was at stake.

"You lose your mother, your father and your little brother," she began gently, "and you don't feel scared about losing the only other member of your family you've got left?"

This seemed to interest Zayad, though his supercilious attitude remained. "Explain further."

"Sakir has lost everyone he's trusted and loved. He takes off from the only home he's ever known and hasn't spoken to the one remaining member of his family in years. Why?" She waited for him to say something, but he didn't. "It can't be just because he's angry with you. He could be angry with you from here. He went halfway around the world, Zayad. Think about it."

Zayad looked thoroughly perplexed.

"If something happened to you," Rita explained.

"He wouldn't be around—he wouldn't be here—to feel it. If he despises you, if he convinces himself that you're responsible for Hassan's death, he won't feel the pain of losing another family member if that should happen."

Zayad shook his head. "How do you know this? Has he said—"

"He's never come out and admitted such a thing. He has too much pride."

Zayad nodded, his eyes deep with understanding.

Rita took a breath. "But I know him. I know what's going on inside him."

"And you love him."

It was a statement, not a question, but Rita felt herself nod.

Zayad was quiet for a moment, his fingers playing with the beads of water inching their way down the sides of his crystal tumbler. Then he turned back to her. "I must speak to him of this."

"No, you can't," Rita insisted, coming to her feet. "He would never forgive me for talking to you about this."

Zayad threw up his hands. "What would you have me do, then?"

"Just try and understand him. For now. Please." Her gaze implored him. "Know that he cares for you and this country more than you'll ever know. Know that in time, he'll make peace with you and with the past."

His jaw tight, Zayad said, "He must."

As Rita walked away from the formidable Sultan of Emand, she hoped to God she hadn't made the biggest mistake of her life. She hoped that her concern for Sakir's heart, and his future with his homeland, people and family hadn't driven her to create more problems, when all she'd wanted to do was make peace.

He had spent the day in meetings with members of Emand Oil's environmental group. But that hadn't stopped Sakir's mind from conjuring images of her, of last night, of this morning.

His chest went tight, as did the rest of him, as he took the palace steps two at a time. Anticipation filled him. More than anything, he wanted to be with Rita—alone, naked, fulfilled. But he would have to be content with seeing her face, perhaps kissing her sweet mouth, and postponing all sensual pleasures until later. His brother was expecting them for dinner tonight.

A frown threatened his good humor as he strode the hallway, but he forced his anger at Zayad away. He was going to her now. Yes, that had his smile returning full force.

He chuckled. Never in his life had he experienced such a pull. They were like moon to tide.

He chuckled once again at the foolish thought, his hand on the doorknob. He would do well to abandon all pangs of romance, concentrate on the real reason he was here in Emand.

Impossible.

When he opened the door, candlelight, driving music and the sensual scent of vanilla met him. The shot of anticipation from a moment ago intensified and all puny thoughts of work disappeared.

There were fifty or so candles in small glass jars lighting a pathway through the suite. Like Hansel and Gretel, a very curious Sakir walked the pathway, all the way through the living room, into the bedroom and out onto the large private terrace.

After that, Sakir noticed nothing. No candles, no scents or sounds. No desert or wind or falling stars.

Nothing but the half-naked woman before him.

Dressed in the native costume of an Emand Saka dancer, Rita smiled coyly at him. "Good evening, Your Highness."

He nodded. "Yes, I would say that it is."

With just that beautiful and highly seductive smile, she took his hand and forced him to sit down in a chair at the table.

The desert breeze blew around them, and he only noticed because it blew the blue gauzy skirt up her amazing thighs.

He licked his lips.

Then she began to dance.

A slow, swaying movement that only the ancient women of the Saka knew. How she was able to learn the dance, he knew not—nor did he care at that moment, for the music was enveloping the space, the sway of her hips was turning his brain to water and everything below his waist to rock-hard need.

Sakir was famished. Not for the wine or the olives and sweetmeats on the plate before him, but for the woman who danced with such abandon—her waist so small, her barely covered breasts rising and falling, her face so happy as she stared at him.

"Rita, please…" He stood, held out his hand. "I have had all I can take."

She grinned, danced to him, thrust out her right hip playfully. "You do not enjoy the dance, Your Highness?"

His gaze went lethal. "I enjoy it very much, Princess."

"But?"

He growled, warned her again. "Rita…"

"I have prepared a few hors d'oeuvres before dinner," she said, then asked coyly, "Are you not hungry?"

Sakir picked her up and slung her over his shoulder. "Famished."

Rita laughed.

At least until he had her on the bed, that filmy skirt up to her waist, her panties down to her ankles—and his tongue in a most heavenly spot.

Thirteen

Rita woke up beside her husband and smiled with happiness. Just lying there, with his nude, dark and heavily muscled body mashed deliciously up against her own, she felt like sighing.

Sakir made her feel so young and sexy and thankful to be alive. All those years of wishing that her gorgeous boss would notice her—or, if we're getting real about it, take her in his arms and make mad, passionate love to her—had not been in vain.

That wish had certainly come true.

For how long, she wasn't certain. But she was content with that. Had to be. She had gone into this love affair with her eyes wide open and she refused to act sad and worried about a future she couldn't control. She would enjoy right now, every moment.

"Good morning."

So intent on her thoughts, Rita hadn't noticed that Sakir was awake and staring at her.

His green eyes nearly drank her in. "What shall we do today?"

She bent down, nuzzled his neck. "We could always do more of this."

A husky moan eased from his throat. "I would be honored, Princess."

"But, then again…" She smiled.

Sakir paused, glanced up, his brow arched. "What are you thinking of?"

With the excitement of a little kid, Rita jumped on top of him, straddled him, grabbed his hands and squeezed. "I want to take you somewhere."

Falling easily into her play, Sakir grinned. "We can go anywhere in the world you wish."

"No, I mean here, in Emand. There's something I have to show you."

"How could this be? You do not know Emand—"

She leaned forward, her face just inches from his. "I'm full of surprises, Your Highness, you should know that by now."

He pulled her to him, kissed her on the mouth. "I do not like surprises."

She chuckled. "Why is that?"

"I wish to know the outcome at all times."

"You can't possibly know the outcome every time."

"I said it is my wish."

Her smile wide, she leaned down again, brushed her lips across his. "Sakir," she whispered, then gave him a thorough kiss—one hot, wet, teasing kiss that lasted a good thirty seconds. Her skin warmed and she thought herself very powerful as she felt him hard and jutting against her thigh. Finally, she sat up and asked, "You want to be in control, is that what it is?"

His eyes burned with the fire of a man who needed release. "Perhaps."

She took his hands and spread his arms back over his head. "Letting others take control now and then can be a very pleasant experience, you know?"

He lifted his head, opened his mouth and ran his tongue across her nipple. "You must convince me further."

Rita sucked in a breath at the intense pleasure of his touch. Her body tight with electricity, she gave him a decadent smile. "Well, our adventure can wait an hour or so."

Sakir grinned, tightened his grip on her. "You are a wise and wonderful woman, Rita Al-Nayhal."

His words swam over her, but she didn't analyze them. She was too busy melting as Sakir lifted his head, took her nipple into his mouth, suckled…

"You may be wise and wonderful, but you are also a reckless driver." The comment came from Sakir, who was now sitting in the passenger side of a black SUV, fully dressed and masked with that I-am-royalty-and-above-it-all attitude.

Rita felt the need to correct him. "I am a confident driver, you mean."

He fairly snorted. "No, I believe reckless is the correct description." He shook his head. "I should have never allowed you to—"

"Allowed me?" she began with mock severity.

"After this driving experience, yes—allowed." He threw his hands up. "When we made that turn back there the car was suspended on two wheels—"

"Oh, c'mon."

"Did you not almost hit that bush right afterward?"

"I tapped it a little bit."

"If I was tapped like that, I would be dead."

She turned and looked at him, then burst out laughing. He followed suit with a rather carefree chuckle.

Rita turned back to the desert road. Was it possible that the sober, always-in-control, rarely-found-life-amusing Sakir Al-Nayhal had changed? And in her care?

Was she too bold to think that she had something to do with this new light and loving side of him? And if she did have something to do with it, would she be responsible for bringing it out of him always—like back in Paradise, back home—

She mentally rolled her eyes. That was a ridiculous thought, not to mention an incredibly sneaky way of allowing herself to hope for a future, a way to stay near and dear to the man she was desperately in love with.

"Are we almost at our destination, Rita?"

She smiled at him. "Be patient."

"Impossible."

She laughed. "Just give it your best shot, all right?"

It was barely ten minutes later when Rita pulled over to the side of the road. Sure, it had been a long drive, but to her, the journey had definitely been worth it. Lord, just for the view alone.

The beautiful Bari Mountains stretched out before her. She took a deep breath and smiled. This land never ceased to amaze her. Mountains and deserts and the palm tree forest and waterfalls. Oh, how much she would love to bring her sister and father here.

She stopped herself from traveling farther with that thought. Emand belonged to Sakir and his family, which she was not part of—not really.

"Let's go," she called cheerfully, grabbing a pack out of the back of the SUV.

"Are we to hike?" Sakir asked, his gaze filled with interest as he took the pack from her.

She liked to see him this way, anticipation on his face. "Just a ways. Our spot is over there, in the flatlands."

Rita was happy to note that the walk wasn't all that rugged, but very pretty. Juniper woodlands encompassed the high flat plains, along with acacia trees and milkweed shrubs. Eagles soared overhead, playing chicken with the cliff faces just below.

Finally, they came to the spot Tureen, one of the sultan's men, had told her about—a rich, well preserved valley floor with a stream, several beautiful old acacia trees and one massive fig tree.

When Rita stopped, Sakir followed suit. "I have never been to this part of the Bari Mountains before."

Rita grinned. "I know."

He frowned, but humor burned behind his eyes. "I do not like this…this secrecy, going behind my back."

On a laugh, Rita grabbed his hand and pulled him toward the surprise she'd been planning since they'd returned from the palm tree forest. "Oh, just relax, Your Highness, and come with me. You'll like it plenty when you see where we're going."

In just under a minute, they stood before it.

Rita turned to watch Sakir's face as he took in the most enormous fig tree in Emand, or so Tureen had told her. His eyes widened and his mouth curved into a handsome smile. With great care, he reached up, cupped a giant piece of ripe, black fruit that hung from the tree's large puzzle-like leafs.

She squeezed his hand. "I thought a picnic under this tree. Bread, cheese, fruit, a little wine. And all we have to do is reach up for dessert."

Sakir said nothing, and she wondered for a moment if he was displeased or worse, unmoved by her sentiment. But after a moment, he turned to her, pulled her into his arms and whispered against her hair. "How did you know?"

"You told me." She pulled back slightly, looked into his eyes. "Don't you remember?"

He blinked, no doubt trying to recall a time when he'd allowed himself to be so open with another human being.

His hands threaded her hair. "Why would you do such a thing for me?"

She smiled a little sadly, stared up at the man of her dreams, knowing full well that she couldn't tell him how much she loved him. It was as though a hand fisted around her heart, but she managed a clear, "I don't know."

"You don't know?" he said, his gaze warm, safe.

She shrugged, not willing to believe she was ever safe enough with him to tell him the truth about her feelings. "I guess I thought you'd like to see it, that's all."

"I do." He smiled. "You are amazing, Rita."

"I hope that doesn't end with 'and any man would be lucky to have you.'" She gave him a playful grin.

He lowered his head, kissed her on the mouth. A soft, tender kiss—not heated as it was this morning. "This is true. Any man *would* be lucky to have you."

The ultrafeminine genes that dwelled within her sprung to life and she wanted to ask him if he would be that man. That lucky one. But she stopped herself, for she wasn't sure if she wanted the answer.

Not now, anyway.

And not here, in this perfect setting.

There would be enough time for truths, she knew. And although she hated to admit it, in her heart she was hoping that with all this time they were spending together, perhaps Sakir would knock down his wall of anger and resentment and embrace a future with her, fall as deeply in love with her as she was with him.

It was, of course, wishful thinking. But hopes could not be helped.

Sakir reached up again. This time, he picked that luscious, black fig from the tree and brought it down between them.

"Have you had a fig from Emand, Rita?"

"Never."

"The taste is unlike anything you have ever known. It is pure and it is pleasure."

Rita's breath caught in her throat. He could be speaking of them, of their time here—of her love for him.

She grinned.

Sakir did, too. "Open your mouth for me."

Resisting the fruit seemed foolish, but resisting Sakir seemed futile. She did as he asked and sighed as warm, sweet fruit met her tongue.

When Sakir and Rita returned to the palace later that day, happy, full and sexually content, there was a message waiting for them.

A message that tossed their relaxed and carefree mood right out of the palace's extravagant floor-to-ceiling windows.

It was from Asad Qahhar and asked for the prince to return his call at his earliest convenience. A deep sense of regret filled Sakir's blood as he left Rita in their suite and went up to his offices in the tower. He was not ready to hear the man's answer, nor was he ready for his time with Rita to end. But in his life, business always came first.

The call took just five minutes, but the outcome brought Sakir little happiness. He was slow in traveling back down to the suite, uncharacteristically awkward as he sat beside Rita on the bed. She was taking off her shoes, looking very content after a day filled with food, figs and lovemaking. He too had felt such contentment.

Until just a moment ago.

When reality had returned.

"Qahhar wishes to meet with us tomorrow afternoon," Sakir said at long last. "He has made his decision."

Rita looked up, her brows knit together. "So soon?"

"I'm afraid so."

She exhaled heavily, her shoes all but forgotten now. "I thought we'd have more time."

"As did I."

The air rushed from Sakir's lungs in a melancholy wheeze. What the devil was wrong with him? He did not understand the depths of his own feeling. This was what he had wanted, what he had come home for. He was poised, ready to take what Qahhar was about to offer him. Hell, he had heard as much in the man's voice. No secretary calling. The man himself, sounding very pleased.

And yet Sakir could muster no excitement.

The thrill of the chase had always been a pleasant one, but it was the capture that truly pleased him.

Not today.

A vise fisted his chest. He did not want to examine the reasons—*or reason*. He did not dare.

"Well," Rita began, a forced enthusiasm to her tone. "A positive and very profitable answer from Qahhar is why we came to Emand, right?"

"It is." No, he reminded himself, she could not read his thoughts. But it was as though she had.

She looked over at him, her eyes filled with questions. But she only asked one. And a general one, at that. "So after we get his decision, we could go back home?"

Sakir nodded. "Perhaps as early as tomorrow night."

Rita said nothing, just gave him a tight-lipped smile. Sakir wanted Rita to force his hand, remind him of their lovemaking, remind him of their time together, remind him that if he were an honorable man he would ask her to be with him—to make their "union" a true and honest state.

But he would not ask for this, just as he knew Rita would not. For very different reasons, of course—where he could never give love to another, Rita was far too proud to ask it of him.

"Do you want me to call him in the morning?" she asked, her back straight, her countenance one of a good and solid business assistant. "Confirm our meeting?"

Sakir put his hand on hers. "Thank you, but no, I will make the call."

With amazing warmth, Rita covered his hand with her remaining one and squeezed.

The action nearly tore Sakir apart.

Where, hours ago, this woman had been his—body, heart and soul—she now had once again become his assistant. He hated the fact, but knew he could have it no other way.

He released her, then stood up, bowed. "I will leave you to get ready for bed."

"Where are you going?" she asked.

"I think I will take a walk in the garden."

"Would you like some company?"

The muscles in his body tensed. He looked down, into her eyes and wanted to get lost there, wanted to say yes. Hell, if he had his preference, he would stay right here, in this bed. But such dreams were impractical. If he continued this impossible romance now, he would not be just a careless rogue, he would be a heartless one.

Rita deserved far more than that.

"I should like to go alone."

She nodded, but stopped him as he turned to walk away. "You know, Sakir," she said, her voice alive with passion. "What you're looking for isn't in that garden. And it's not in an eighty-hour workweek or a sprawling ranch in Texas."

He stopped, but didn't turn around.

"God, I hope you find it."

His jaw tight, he asked, "Find what?"

"Whatever it is that's going to make you happy and fulfilled." She paused, took a breath. "I'd truly love to see you that way."

Anger surged into Sakir, but at what—at whom— he was not sure. Madness had come over him the moment he had stepped onto his plane with this woman beside him.

Did she not understand?

He did not care for happiness and fulfillment. They were fleeting. No, he wanted only to find sanity again.

A muscle twitched beneath his right eye, but he ignored the uncontrolled movement, stuck out his chin proudly and walked out of the room.

Fourteen

The time was 1:00 p.m.

The place: the grand library in the sultan's palace.

Beautifully bound books swelled to the rafters; leather sofas and chairs were dotted about atop silk carpets to make the space a comfortable one; gold and marble tables held platters of cakes and cookies, while in the royal china were full servings of hot Turkish coffee.

It was glorious, and very overwhelming for the laymen, a class to which Rita and Emand Oil's Asad Qahhar definitely subscribed.

Rita had not been surprised at Sakir's quick change of venue. He liked the home court advantage, so to speak, when closing a deal. And there was nothing that rivaled the palace, save the White House.

Asad did not lean back in his chair as he had in his own offices in town. No, he remained straight-backed in his posture and deferential in his manner. "I am pleased, Your Highness. Al-Nayhal Corporation will do well for Emand Oil, I am certain of it."

Sakir, who had yet to sit down, nodded from his place behind the sofa. "We look forward to working with you."

"I feel the same," Asad said, then paused. "I cannot tell you how pleased I am that you will be in Emand several times a year. This makes me feel very comfortable in my choice."

Rita could feel Sakir stiffen all the way across the room. Although she didn't have to, she caught the quick glare he sent her way. She wasn't sure what he was going to do here or say to Qahhar. Perhaps he'd ignore the man's comment or amend Rita's previous and imprudent offer from their last meeting. Either way, it would surely quash the deal for them.

"I will be here two or three times per year," Sakir announced, then proceeded to pour himself another cup of coffee.

Rita nearly fell out of her leather armchair and choked on a pecan cookie. Had she heard him right? Had he just agreed to come home several times a year? She had no clue what had brought on such a change of heart, but she vowed to ask him about it later.

Asad nodded. "Two or three times, you say?"

"If this is not sufficient, I am sorry," Sakir said tightly. "But, alas, it is all I will commit to."

Asad shook his head. "No. This is very well, Your Highness. I am very pleased indeed."

"Good." He stuck out his hand. "We have a deal then."

Asad Qahhar stood and the two men shook on it. Rita just stared at them, her brain in some type of fog. She couldn't wait for the older man to leave so she could ask Sakir what had just happened here. And when he did, she pounced on Sakir.

"I don't understand."

"What don't you understand?" Sakir said, still standing, still looking as tight and professional as ever.

"You have agreed to come to Emand several times a year."

"I have."

She rolled her eyes. "Are you going to make me spell this out?"

Sakir sighed. "I did what I had to do to make the deal."

This made her pause. For a moment, just a moment there, she'd thought perhaps he'd really changed. She'd thought that maybe he'd forgiven his brother, wanted to come home again, wanted something different than deals and contracts and work, work, work. But that—again—had been just wishful thinking.

"You did what you had to do for the deal," she repeated. "Just as you did with us, right?"

"Yes," he said tightly. "That is right."

Rita stared at Sakir, her heart bleeding. No longer was he the sensual, carefree man she had known over the last several days. The man she loved and had made love to in her bed. No, the man that stood before her now

was the same man who had left her last night and who
had slept on the couch in their suite.

Her boss.

All business. All the time.

"I must see to some paperwork," he said, then
quickly downed the cup of coffee. "We will see each
other later, yes?"

"Of course." Her heart thoroughly ached, and she
wanted to curl up in her chair with a big, fluffy blanket
and cry for a few hours. But she didn't have that luxury. She had to be all about business as well if she was
to survive this. "Do you need any help with the work?"

"No. Thank you."

It was funny. Even in her anger and frustration, she
wanted to help him. Well, that was love, folks. What
an idiot she was for thinking she could get through this
unscathed.

She watched him walk out of the room, then fell
back against the chair and downed her coffee. She
wanted to take a few minutes, a little time to sit and feel
sorry for herself, but the library suddenly felt very con-
fining and she decided to get up and get out. Once in
the hall, she headed out to the gardens. It seemed the
place for thought and reflection—perhaps even regrets,
if she had a mind to list them.

The morning sun warmed her skin and the desert
breeze cooled her down as she walked along the rows
of roses. She was just bending down to smell a perfectly lovely yellow variety, when someone came up behind her.

"We must talk."

Rita whirled around, nearly stabbing her palm with a thorn in the process. "Zayad. You scared the life out of me."

"I apologize," he said, but didn't look the least bit sorry.

He stood before her, hands behind his back, his handsome face etched with tension as his white caftan whipped in the soft wind. "I know I have agreed to keep silent on the subject of my brother until he is ready, but I can do this no longer."

Rita's heart leapt into her throat. "Why?"

"I know the bargain you have made with Qahhar. This means your business is done here. You will leave Emand very shortly and I will never be able to confront my brother."

Rita's mind whirled with thought. Zayad was right, of course, but if he talked to Sakir now, about what she'd said, Sakir would be livid. He would admonish her for interfering, but he would probably never speak to her again for having his pride crushed before his brother.

She shook her head. "I'm sorry, Zayad, but—"

"I am sorry, too, my sister, but Sakir and I must speak."

"He's got to find his own way back home and to you," she said passionately.

He stood tall before her, his arms crossed over his broad chest. "Are you really asking me to forget all that you have said to me?"

"For now, yes."

"Well, I cannot. I will not." He turned away, his head

high, his manner defiant. Then he turned back. "I brought Sakir here to end this war, not to—"

"What?" The blood in Rita's ears began to pound. "What did you just say?"

Zayad shook his head, his lips thinning dangerously. "I want our family back together. I want my brother to know his place here. I want him back in Emand where he belongs. It is important to all—"

"Stop." Rita couldn't believe she was speaking so boldly, commanding a sultan in his own home, but she was beyond reason. "You *brought* Sakir here?"

Zayad sighed, said nothing for a moment and then, "Yes. I arranged for the meeting between Sakir and Qahhar."

"Oh my God."

"The interest in my brother for Emand Oil was my doing. So what?"

"So what?" she fairly choked out. "You speak of pride and honor. Sakir has these in spades."

"He would come no other way."

She threw her hands up. "He thought he got this all on his own, his talents…"

"It was on his own merit that he landed this account, Rita. Make no mistake. But Qahhar did come to me for counsel, and I gave him my advice. I told him who I believed was the best man for the job."

Above them, a cloud rolled in and covered the sun. The air cooled and the flowers seemed to wilt slightly. Rita swallowed, shook her head. "Sakir is going to be furious when he finds this out."

Zayad lifted his chin. "Just as he would if he knew you discussed his fears of loss regarding his family with me?"

Her belly clenched, she nodded. "Yes."

"Well, it is too late for the both of you, then."

Rita whirled around, her heart in her throat. No, no, no. It wasn't him. Not now.

But her silent plea went unanswered.

Eyes filled with hatred, Sakir stared at her. "From him I would expect such deceit—" he shook his head, his voice brutal "—but never from you, Rita."

Stunned, sickened by his withering gaze, Rita could only shake her head. But aloud, she could take nothing back. The situation before Sakir looked just as it was. Two people discussing him, covering up their previous conversations—conspiring to hold back things he had a right to know.

Rita felt raw, exposed and utterly defeated.

In her hope of helping him, she had deceived him.

"Brother," Zayad began slowly and with much patience.

"We are no longer brothers," Sakir uttered with thick revulsion.

Tears pricked Rita's eyes, but she swiped at them and took a step toward the man she loved. "Sakir, please listen to me—"

He stopped her cold. Full-blown reproach burned in his green eyes. Then, as he'd done earlier that day, he turned and walked away.

Fifteen

Rita Thompson had courage.

It had been a big trait of her mother's. The woman had been known to rise from the ashes in times of crisis, and do what needed to be done—say what needed to be said—regardless of the consequences. And no matter how badly she had wished to escape the discomfort of a confrontation, running away with things left unresolved just hadn't been an option for her.

This had been an invaluable, though difficult, lesson for Rita through the years. But things had always turned out better for it in the end.

She hoped today would be no different.

As she walked into the palace and took the stairs to her room, Rita heard her mother's voice in her head. She was urging her daughter to go to Sakir, apologize for how she'd handled things with Zayad and tell him what was in her heart.

Rita knew full well her regrets would not be taken with any sense of forgiveness, just as she knew her feelings of love would not be reciprocated. But when she arrived at the suite door, she didn't flinch. She turned the knob and went in.

She didn't see Sakir at first, and she wondered if he had gone to another part of the palace and had his things sent to him—or if he was already on his way to the airport. But then he walked out of the bedroom.

He had changed from caftan to jeans and a white shirt. He looked so handsome, so angry, so lost. She wanted to throw herself into his arms and cry her way to absolution, but she was no child. She would handle things as a grown woman, without entreaty and tears.

She swallowed the grapefruit-size lump in her throat and began. "I screwed up. Really screwed up. I'm sorry."

He lifted his chin. "It is forgotten."

Everything in his gaze, everything in his manner, screamed the opposite. "I doubt that."

"The bottom line is I have Emand Oil and you have your partnership. We will focus on this."

His words cut deep. She couldn't care less for the partnership. She wanted him to understand why she did what she did. And if God was handing out miracles, she wanted Sakir to give in to his feelings—feelings she knew in her soul were there, behind the thorny wall around his heart.

She wanted him to love her.

She walked over to him, stood a few feet away. "Sakir, we need to talk. I mean, really talk."

"I have much to do."

"It'll take a minute."

"I have papers to go over before we leave in the morning."

Leave in the morning...

The shock of that statement assailed her, dropped on her heart like a steel weight. Yes, they were getting on a plane tomorrow.

Back to real life.

Back to Paradise, Texas, and working and living under the pretense that this whole marriage—the nights of lovemaking and the days of friendship—had been a sham.

Rita took a deep breath. "Fine, but at least hear me out before you go."

He clipped her an impersonal nod. "Speak then, but understand, my heart is lost to you."

Pain seared into her soul at his words. But she knew she had to say what she'd come here to say. Sakir needed to hear it. He needed to hear the truth.

"The people of this country love you," she said. "Your brother loves you. And I love you."

His eyes blazed green fire; his nostrils flared.

Rita released a shaky breath. "I understand your fears about losing those you care about. The pain is unimaginable, I know—"

"You do not know anything," he replied in a voice taut with fury.

"I lost my mother when I was young, Sakir," she countered vehemently. "Believe me, I know."

This statement stopped him cold. For a moment, the ire on his face dropped away and genuine interest took its place. For once, perhaps he was thinking about her family and not his own painful history.

"I am sorry about your mother," he said at long last.

"Thank you."

"But it is different."

She agreed. "I know. When she died I was very angry, but I didn't blame anyone else for her death."

Rage filtered back into his gaze. His glanced at the door. "What more have you to say?"

What more besides, "I love you."

The midmorning sun inched its way into the room from the terrace windows, bathing both her and Sakir in its light.

"I went to your brother because I care about you," Rita explained.

Sakir scoffed at this.

"You can believe it or not. But it's the truth." She cocked her head, tried to get through to him with words and eyes filled with tenderness. "You needed the help, the push, whatever you want to call it—you needed it to get past this darkness you live in."

Through gritted teeth, Sakir uttered, "I needed no help. Especially regarding Zayad."

"Don't make the mistake of pushing him out of your life again," she said, her tone imploring him to listen. "He's all the family you have left."

Something close to vulnerability shone in Sakir's eyes at that declaration.

"If you do," Rita continued, "you'll regret it for as long as you live."

"I do not indulge in regret, Rita." He lifted a brow. "For anything or anyone."

Rita exhaled heavily. "You can toss out all these self-righteous one-liners and pretend none of this matters to you, but I know better."

"How is it you know?" he bated.

"I know because I see you, Sakir. I see you and your heart."

His green eyes narrowed and hardened. "Just because we fell into bed a handful of times does not mean you know who I am."

Rita felt as if she'd been stabbed. Her stomach threaded into knots and she could hardly catch her breath. No one had ever said something so cruel to her. Out of pain, fear, resentment—it didn't matter. Sakir had crossed a line today and no matter what happened, things between them would never be the same again.

Just as she would never be the same again.

He stared at her, still proud and unaffected. "Is there anything more you wish to say?"

"Only this." She mustered up every ounce of aplomb she possessed and looked him straight in the eye. "I quit."

And this time, with a bruised heart and a numb spirit, she was the one who turned and walked away.

* * *

What he needed was a smooth cigar and a very tall glass of whiskey.

Sakir sat in the worn leather chair his father had always used to think on important matters. He'd been cooped up in his father's study in the back section of the palace tower for close to three hours now—doing nothing, saying nothing, trying like hell to erase everything he'd heard and said today.

He was very good at that.

He had erased the past decade from his mind with ease. He had thought one day should be nothing to him.

He had been wrong.

As she had from the first moment they had met, the moment he had kissed her at their wedding altar, the moment he had first slid inside her body and the moment she had taken him in search of figs, Rita Thompson had insinuated herself into his mind and held steady.

He could not get her eyes out of his memory, just as he could not expunge the repulsive words he had uttered to her. Words that had meant to shock, to hurt, to drive away this woman who had come to mean far too much to him.

And he had succeeded.

With eyes filled with pain, she had told him that she would no longer be working in his employ.

Bitter laughter fell from Sakir's lips. He had lost her heart and her mind. And her love…

He growled, let his head fall into his hands.

This was a good thing, the right thing. He did not

want this woman's love. He did not want such a burden. Yet every time he played those four daunting words— *I love you, Sakir*—over in his head, his chest seized and his body ached for her.

He drove his hand through his hair. Dammit, he had been a fool for bringing her here, for making that agreement. Marriage, even one crafted on subterfuge, was a very risky undertaking. And he had taken the leap without a thought. All he had seen was Emand Oil, spurning his brother and getting close to a woman he had longed to touch and taste for years.

In truth, he deserved whatever wounds he got.

All thoughts died right then and there, as suddenly a sword whizzed past his head and dropped onto the table beside him, the steel blade smashing against the wood with a loud clatter.

"Let us resolve this."

Sakir whirled around, saw his brother standing over him and threw him a sneer.

Zayad's grin held no humor, either. In fact, he looked ready to do battle. "Unless all that time in America has left you soft."

Through clenched teeth, Sakir uttered, "You provoke me?"

Zayad inclined his head. "I do."

The anger that raged inside Sakir, the anger that had been eating at him for too many years to count, rushed to the surface in electric currents. His blood pounded in his veins, and his every muscle tensed.

Sakir and his brother had worked with swords for

many years, both excelling at the art. But today, at this moment, they were not playing a child's game. This was a battle, true and without fear.

"Not here." Sakir grabbed the sword and held it to his side. "Not in our father's room."

"Agreed."

Zayad walked out of the room. Sakir followed, his gaze like that of a hawk's. They both knew where they were going. The large terrace that spanned the entire third floor had always been used for formal occasions and state dinners.

Today, it would serve as the field of a final conflict.

The sun glared down on Sakir's back as he walked out onto the stone. But he cared little. His mind and his body were set like an animal's, ready to pounce, to strike. He never looked away from his brother as he positioned himself and waited—for it was the honor of the sultan to begin the match.

Zayad also positioned himself, then without a word he lifted his brow just slightly.

It was enough.

Sakir rushed him, his sword first held high above his head, and then slamming down. Metal crashed against metal.

Zayad's footwork was excellent and Sakir was forced back, back against the balcony wall. But he wasn't about to be defeated so easily. With a grin, he lunged at Zayad. Again, swords clashed as his brother was ready for him and struck back. Hard and heavy.

The sun beat down on them without mercy. Over

and over, back and forth, the two brothers battled. Sweat dripped from Sakir's brow into his eyes, but he allowed the sting to replenish his energy. And he used all the rage that dwelled inside of him.

He blocked and slashed and attacked, sparring with Zayad back almost to the railing.

Suddenly Zayad cried out. Sakir paused, his breathing labored. He watched his brother look down, turn over his hand and stare. Blood dripped from a gash in Zayad's palm.

Zayad looked up and gave Sakir a deadly glare. Again he cried out, but this time it was the cry of a warrior.

Zayad attacked like a man possessed. His sword fell to Sakir's leg, his waist, his chest.

Time seemed to hold still as they battled.

But not for long.

It was Sakir who howled next, who backed off. Blinding pain seized his arm. Blood seeped eagerly from the rip in his white shirt.

He looked at Zayad, his brow raised questioningly. Zayad knew that look, knew what it meant and nodded, sweat dripping from his forehead. Shedding blood was enough for them both; they quit and backed off.

"You have remained quick, brother," Zayad said through weighty breaths.

Sakir pressed the palm of his hand to his wound. "And you have remained slow."

Zayad chuckled and let his sword fall. "Shall we go again, then?"

Sakir shook his head and snorted. "I would like that, but alas I am too old."

Zayad walked to him and then fell to his backside onto the stone floor. "As am I."

Sakir also sat, exhausted. He no longer felt like the man of business, the man of indifference, the man of anger. Sitting here, on the floor with his brother, bleeding and trading gibes, he felt like a child, battled and bruised and ready for a nap.

The brothers sat in silence for a moment, then Zayad knifed a hand through his wet hair and sighed. "I miss Hassan."

Sakir looked away, the pain in his arm nothing to the pain he felt for the loss of his younger brother. "You could have kept him at home."

Zayad wiped the blood from his hand onto the stones beside him. "Sakir, do you not remember our brother?"

"Of course I remember him."

"Then you will recall that while on this earth he was a wild little monkey, a proud eagle—he could not be contained."

Sakir ripped off the sleeve of his shirt and handed it to Zayad for a makeshift bandage. If he thought back, if he allowed himself to think back on his little brother, he would see a boy just as Zayad had described. Hassan had been as stubborn as the rest of them.

Sakir glanced up, nodded. "He was a true son of Al-Nayhal, that is certain."

Grief moved through Zayad's gaze. "But for my son,

we are the last of this family. Can we not resolve our differences and be brothers once more?"

No biting comment found its way to Sakir's lips this time. He had fought a weary battle over the last ten years. Perhaps it was time to throw down his sword and face his fears, accept that his brother had no control over life and death, just as he, Sakir, did not.

"Perhaps we should resolve this," Sakir said with just a touch of humor. "For I fear I could not survive another clash of swords."

Zayad laughed again. It was a good sound. One Sakir had missed, though he would never admit it aloud. Once upon a time, when his mother and father had been alive, the family had sat together, taken a meal and laughed.

It had been a long time ago.

"You will forgive Rita, as well?"

Sakir shot out of the fog of memory and fairly choked. "What do you say?"

"Rita is owed an apology, my brother."

Sakir did not want to hear such a thing. He bit back. "This is none of your affair. And besides, she had no right—"

"She had the right of a wife who loves her husband."

Sakir snorted with derision. "Wife. She is not my—" He stopped short, stared at his brother. "But I gather you already knew that."

Zayad's brows knit together. "I thought I did. I thought your marriage was not based on love. But now I am not so sure."

"What does that mean?" Sakir asked, irritated.

"You may have married her out of necessity, brother, but much has changed, yes?"

Sakir opened his mouth to speak, to refute his brother's claim, then promptly shut it. Although he did not care to confess such foolishness on his part, he could not deny the change in his feelings, either.

He had married Rita to have respectability with his conservative clients, yes. But somewhere between the plane ride to Emand and the palm tree forest, things had turned and morphed into a genuine affection.

Zayad glanced down at his wounded hand. "Pride will keep you from this woman you love."

"Love," Sakir said with much flippancy. "What do I know of love?"

"Not much, that is true. But I am a man with eyes. I see how you look at one another." He grinned. "There is much feeling there."

"Bah."

Zayad placed his wounded hand on his brother's shoulder. "Sakir, will you do something for me?"

"What is it?"

"For one moment, think of your life without her."

It was as though he had been stuck by his brother's sword once again. But the words Zayad had uttered were far more painful than a mere nick on the arm.

His life without Rita.

But no, he would not be without her, he reminded himself. She would be at his side, his partner in the firm. All day they would be together. Then, of course, at night they would go their separate ways; she to her home and he to his—

Sakir stopped right there.

There would be no working together. He would not see her.

She had quit her job.

Under the hot sun, Sakir felt deathly cold. Even when Rita had told him that she quit, he did not think it possible. He did not think of her as gone, out of his life and his bed. Forever.

He lifted his head to the heavens and cursed into the wild desert air.

"It is as I thought." Zayad gave him a brotherly rap on the arm.

A sharp sting bit at Sakir and he let fly a groan.

Zayad chuckled. "Sorry, brother. But as you have already seen, no pain compares to the loss of a woman's favor."

"That may very well be." Sakir shook his head. "But it matters little now."

"Why?"

"I have said foolish, malicious things to her."

Zayad stood, offered his brother a hand. "She will forgive you."

The look in Rita's eyes this morning spoke differently. Yes, Sakir knew there was still love there. But she was clearly resigned to his snarls and her decision. Resignation was far worse than being angry.

Sakir grabbed his brother's hand. "She would refuse me now."

Zayad pulled Sakir to his feet. "I think not."

"You do not know her as I do."

Zayad shrugged. "You give in, then?"

One word sat on Sakir's tongue, refusing to stir. "Never."

Sixteen

She would miss this place.

Rita stared out the airport's soaring windows at the desert in the distance. The sun was slowly setting, tossing that exquisite pinky-peach glow her way, making her smile a little sadly. In a million years, she'd never have thought that she'd become as attached to this land as she had. Heck, she was supposed to be a Texan through and through. But Emand had snagged her heart.

Just as its sheikh had.

Her heart squeezed, but she forced the feeling away. She'd have to get used to this empty feeling. She'd have to remember that she had no Sakir, no job, no romance. She was going home with nothing, with only the hope of rebuilding her life. Thank goodness her sister Ava's wedding was just a few short weeks away. Getting lost in last-minute wedding details, helping the nervous bride with her makeup and dress would surely keep Rita's mind occupied. Then when Ava and Jared finally left for their honeymoon, Rita would get to work on finding a new job.

"Flight Fourteen to Paris, France, en route to Dallas, Texas, will be boarding at Gate Six."

Rita didn't even glance up when her flight was called. She'd booked a commercial flight back to the States, with a short layover in Paris. She hadn't told Sakir she was leaving, as she sure didn't want to ride back with him.

Her stomach clenched. Just the thought of hours on a plane with the man who had rejected her…it would be way too humiliating.

"All first-class passengers traveling on Flight Fourteen to Paris, France, en route to Dallas, Texas, should be boarding at this time."

Rita flipped through her magazine not even seeing the pictures. She didn't want to run in the direction of the gateway, not just yet. She had a little time, sure, but it wasn't that. The truth was she wanted to hold on to Emand and the memories she'd made here for as long as possible.

A fact that made her want to kick herself.

Oh, well. Soon enough she'd be on that plane, climbing into her snug little coach seat and flying home.

Back to Paradise.

Rita smiled a little sadly. Right now, her hometown

sounded like just that—heaven for a woman who felt like hell.

Unbidden, an image of she and Sakir making love, laughing underneath that massive fig tree, popped into her head.

Her throat ached with unshed tears. How could she have been so stupid? Thinking all the time that a future with this man never mattered, that all those wonderful days and nights and moments and memories would just fade into the scrapbook of her mind—forget the emotions that had come with them.

Well, Rita. That's what you get for marrying the boss. Boss…

She shook her head, feeling unbelievably defeated. After today, Sakir would no longer be her boss. She'd quit, and no matter how hard it was going to be to find a new job, there was no way she was going back to Al-Nayhal Corporation. She couldn't see Sakir again and work with him every day, as her heart continued to pine and to break.

"At this time we would like to invite all coach passengers traveling on Flight Fourteen to Paris, France, en route to Dallas, Texas, to board."

On legs of water, Rita stood up, her carry-on feeling like it was filled with boulders as she walked slowly toward the terminal.

"Where has she gone?"

Sakir stood over Gana, who, up until a moment ago, had been stripping the sheets on the bed he had shared with Rita just a few nights ago. Zayad was beside him, not saying much, just giving his brother the support he had claimed he did not need.

The young woman bowed low. "I do not know, Your Highness."

"She said nothing?" he demanded, his arms crossed over his chest—a chest that had been constricting every time he thought about Rita leaving the palace, leaving him without a word.

"She embraced me, Your Highness. Thanked me for my service."

Sakir could barely contain his frustration, but he forced calm into his voice. "Think Gana, please. She packed her clothes—"

"The princess left most of her clothing, Your Highness," Gana said quickly.

A cold knot twisted in Sakir's belly. Of course she would not take his gifts. She was far too proud to take from him after what had happened, after what he had said to her. "Fine," he said tightly. "She packed the clothes she brought to Emand then, and…?"

The woman looked up to the ceiling, sniffed, clearly racking her brain for more of an answer than "I do not know." Finally, her weary gaze returned to his. "I am sorry, Your Highness."

Zayad, who had remained quiet up until now, stepped forward. "Did she want to travel to the mountains again? Perhaps tour the deserts?"

The young woman took a deep breath, shook her

head. "Not that I am aware of, Your Royal Highness." Her brow furrowed then. "Wait a moment."

"What is it?" Sakir demanded.

"There was one thing she said that sounded strange."

Zayad looked ready to shake the maid. "Well, out with it, Gana."

The young woman's eyes widened. "It was about the French."

"The French?" Sakir repeated. "What the devil does that mean?"

"She asked me if I thought the people in France call their string potatoes *French fries* as she would in America."

Zayad grinned at the amusing query, said to his brother, "She means to leave Emand."

Sakir nodded, his gut tight. Routes back to the States on commercial airlines went regularly through London and Paris. Odds were that she was at the airport this minute, or already on her way out of the country.

On his way up to the suite moments ago, he had thought that perhaps she had made her way to the airport. But he had not been certain and did not want to alert the airport security, and whoever else might be listening in, of a missing Emand princess.

Sakir walked to the open balcony and looked out. His heart pounded wildly in his chest; his mouth felt dry as the desert beyond. Never in his life had he been so afraid to lose something, someone. He had been a fool to hold on to the past with an iron fist. Now he was paying the price.

"Sakir?"

He turned. His brother raised a brow in unspoken query. *What to do?*

Well, he would not let her leave, certainly. Not until he had said what was on his mind and on his heart. Odds were good she would refuse him, but if he did not see her one last time, apologize and profess his truths, he would lose not only the woman he loved, but his sanity as well.

"Shall I call for the car?" Zayad asked.

Sakir nodded, reached in his pocket and took out his cell phone. "But first, I will speak to my men at the airport."

"Rita Al-Nayhal?"

The man who had spoken her name so quietly and with such reverence stood before her, his head inclined slightly. He was joined at the hip with a far larger man, very bodyguard-esque in his searching eyes, meaty fists and tight-lipped mouth.

"It's Rita Thompson, actually," she corrected, her heart dipping just a bit as she said the words.

The man didn't acknowledge her amendment, just said very seriously, "Would you follow me, ma'am?"

"I'm about to get on a plane." She shook her head, confused. "Is there some problem?"

"No problem at all, ma'am." The man lowered his voice once more. "There are a few security measures for members of the Al-Nayhal family that we must adhere to."

Rita opened her mouth to reiterate that she was no longer a member of the family, but the man said far too quickly, "We have changed the gate for your flight, that is all, and wish to escort you there."

A shiver inched up Rita's spine and she turned. She saw many of her fellow passengers stopping where a woman collected boarding passes and stamped their tickets before they went through to the gate. "I don't think so. This is my plane right here. It's going to Paris, then to Texas."

"Your Highness, we do not wish to make a scene."

"Neither do I. And by the way, how do you know who I am?"

"We are security, ma'am," was all he offered. "It is important for you to come with us."

Panic shot through Rita's blood. "I'm not going anywhere with you people."

Just then, the bodyguard stepped forward. He said nothing, but he didn't have to. He was pretty imposing. The smallish man continued to speak, "You will come with us, ma'am." He lifted a brow. "*How* you come with us is entirely up to you."

Anxiety turned to anger inside of Rita. She knew who was behind this. Her "husband." No doubt, Sakir had called the airport and was having her sent back to the palace.

Why, she didn't know. He didn't want her anymore.

She eyed the bodyguard, knew she couldn't take him down or run from him, so she acquiesced. But she knew that when she got back to the palace, she was going to give that arrogant sheikh a piece of her mind.

The two men escorted her through the airport and

down several hallways. Soon the exit to the airport came into view, but the men didn't lead her in that direction.

"Where are we going?" she demanded, fear twisting in her blood.

"To your plane, ma'am."

"My plane—" she began, then paused.

There it was, sitting pretty outside the floor-to-ceiling windows.

Sakir's plane.

Of course.

A deep sadness filled her, and a lump formed in her throat. Sakir wasn't bringing her back to the palace for a chat. He was letting her leave. No fight. He just wanted to make sure she left in the same way she'd come—safe and sound and in style.

As if that mattered to her at all.

But no one was going to accuse Sakir Al-Nayhal of not being a gentleman.

Rita lifted her chin and proudly walked out into the sunshine, onto the tarmac and up the steps of the plane. A week ago, she'd come down these steps with a light heart and a wave of excitement.

What a heartbreaking turnaround.

When she entered the body of the plane, Rita felt thankful to leave the jerk security guys behind and to see the same flight attendant who had worked on her last flight over to Emand.

The man bowed to her and gave a warm, "Welcome aboard, Your Highness."

"I'm not a 'Your Highness' any more," she said drily.

The man only inclined his head.

"Can I take any seat?" she asked, just wanting to curl up in a ball and pray for sleep to hit her.

"The sheikh has requested your presence in the back of the plane, Your Highness."

She rolled her eyes. "Well, you can just tell the sheikh to go—"

She stopped short, her brows knitting together.

The sheikh requested...

Oh, God, no.

Her heart slamming against her ribs, she struggled to think of what to do next. She didn't want to see him and she sure as hell couldn't let him see her—not with love still shining in her eyes.

"Where is it that I should go, Rita?"

Rita stood stock-still, letting that voice seep into her heart and soul like honey and chocolate. If she wasn't as strong as she was, there would be nothing to stop her from running to him and throwing her arms around his neck.

But she was strong.

She turned around and faced him. As always, he looked too gorgeous for words, casually dressed in jeans and a black shirt. "What are you doing here?"

"We came here together. We will leave together."

"Honestly, there's no need to act all chivalrous," she said rigidly. "You should go home, back to the palace, to your people, where you belong—and let me go home to Paradise, where I belong."

His eyes were intense and passion-filled. "You do not belong in Paradise."

She sniffed. "More than I do here, that's for sure."

"I do not agree."

"Sakir," she said quickly, done with all this small talk. "What am I doing here? What do you want?"

"When did your mother die, Rita?"

Rita sucked in a breath, the question taking her completely by surprise. Tears filled her eyes and she choked out, "What?"

Sakir shook his head. "I am sorry that I never asked about her, about the pain you must have experienced in losing her." He shrugged sadly. "I was caught up in my own history—too caught up to see anything else."

Confusion spun in Rita's mind. "I don't understand. Why are you doing this? It's—"

"Important?"

"No. No, it's cruel." She took a step toward him, her voice breaking. "Don't pretend to care about me now. It's over, okay? I'm fine. There's no need to apologize, or have regrets." She threw her hands in the air. "No harm done."

His eyes filled with tenderness and with disbelief.

She sighed and sagged a little. "Well, maybe that's not entirely true, but I'll get over it." She paused and said words that were killing her to say. "I'll get over you."

"I do not wish for you to get over me."

"Why is that? So I'll stay at Al-Nayhal Corporation?"

"I will not pretend that you remaining in my company is not important to me, but it is nothing to having you beside me in other ways." His gaze went soft, tender. "In my arms, my bed, my heart."

Rita just stared, a flicker of hope winding its way though her. "Sakir…"

"Please come to me." He held a hand out to her.

She shook her head.

"Why?" he asked.

"I don't believe you. I don't believe any of this."

"And?"

"And…" Her throat was so tight. "I'm afraid."

"Of what, Rita?"

"Your words. They hurt too much."

He frowned. "I know. God, I know. I am beside myself with shame for what I have said to you. It was wrong and wholeheartedly untrue. My only excuse is one of fear. I knew I had fallen in love with you. I thought the only way I could regain my power was to hurt you." He shook his head, drew a jagged breath. "I was a coward, Rita."

Rita held her breath; on the verge of tears, she thought she'd bust out at any moment. She didn't know what to think, what to believe. She loved this man so much she ached with it. But she was so afraid; her heart couldn't take another rejection.

"Words can hurt, dearest," he said with supreme tenderness in his tone. "But they can also heal. I know this because my brother and I have talked and reconciled."

"You have?" she said, overcome with astonishment. "But I thought—"

"You thought I was a fool who would continue to hold my brother responsible for a life he had no control over in the first place just to protect myself against further pain."

"Yes."

"I am a new man, Rita." Sakir grinned, his eyes filled with warmth. "You have made me thus. Just as you have given Zayad and me a new beginning. Make no mistake, dearest. We both know that it was you who brought our family back together."

Tears spilled from Rita's eyes. She shook her head. "No."

"Yes, dearest." Again, he held his hand out to her. "I want to thank you. And if you will let me, I want to give you the family you have given me."

"Sakir…"

"Forgive me. Please."

Rita could hardly say the word. All the emotion, all the love in her heart had settled in her throat. But she couldn't help herself. She felt herself nod, felt herself running to him, wrapping her arms around his neck, sighing as she felt him so strong and safe and real.

He nuzzled her neck and whispered in her ear, "Thank you."

She clung to him.

"I love you, my dearest," he said.

"And I love you," Rita said breathlessly.

Sakir pulled back just an inch, dipped his head and covered her mouth with his. His kiss was tender at first, so loving and open. But it quickly grew heated and sensual, his mouth moving over hers as he murmured words of love she'd longed for, hoped for and wished to hear.

After a few moments, he eased his mouth from hers, though his gaze remained steadfast, true and so open at long last.

"Dearest?"

"Yes?" she said, loving this new and heartfelt endearment he was calling her.

Sakir lowered to one knee, grinned up at her. "I ask for your hand in marriage."

She gave a chirp of laughter. "Again?"

"This time, I will do things properly."

With a grin, he opened a small box. Rita looked down and snaked in a breath. An enormous pink diamond winked up at her.

"Will you have me?" he asked.

"Oh, Sakir, always and forever." She smiled at him, watched and held her breath as he slipped the ring on her finger.

Just a short time ago, she had been standing at an altar with a man who knew no love, no forgiveness and no true happiness. Because she wanted him and believed in him, she had been willing to go with him, see a different side of life, experience new and exciting adventures.

Sakir stood then, kissed her softly on the mouth and then hauled her to him.

Around them, the engines of the plane roared to life. The sound was a metaphor for them and for new beginnings.

Rita melted into Sakir's arms, knowing deep in her soul that she'd found all that she'd been looking for— her ideal husband, her loyal fiancé, her one true love and so many magnificent adventures to come.

* * * * *

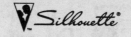

COMING NEXT MONTH

#1609 THE LAWS OF PASSION—Linda Conrad
Dynasties: The Danforths
When attorney Marcus Danforth was falsely arrested, FBI agent
Dana Aldrich rushed to prove his innocence. Brought together by the
laws of the court, they discovered their intense mutual attraction ignited
the laws of passion. Yet Dana wanted more from this sizzling-hot lawyer—
she wanted love.…

#1610 CAUGHT IN THE CROSSFIRE—Annette Broadrick
The Crenshaws of Texas
The arousing connection between blue-eyed Jared Crenshaw and
Lindsey Russell was undeniable from the moment they met. Before he
knew it, Jake had woken up in Lindsey's bed, but how had he gotten there?
He was certain they'd been caught in the crossfire of somebody's scandalous
scheme.…

#1611 LOST IN SENSATION—Maureen Child
Mantalk
Dr. Sam Holden was still reeling from the past when Tricia Wright swept
him up into a whirlwind of passion. This woman was an intriguing force of
nature: blond, bubbly and hot as hell. But their joint future was put
permanently on hold until he could conquer the past that haunted him.

#1612 DARING THE DYNAMIC SHEIKH—Kristi Gold
The Royal Wager
Princess Raina Kahlil had no desire to marry the man she'd been promised
to. That was until she met Sheikh Dharr Ibn Halim face-to-dashingly-
handsome-face. While Raina found herself newly drawn to her culture and
country, she was even more intensely drawn to its future king.…

#1613 VERY PRIVATE DUTY—Rochelle Alers
The Blackstones of Virginia
Federal agent Jeremy Blackstone was the only man Tricia Parker had ever
loved. Now, years after they'd parted, she was nursing him back to health.
Tricia struggled not to fall under Jeremy's sensual spell, but how could she
resist playing the part of both nurse *and* lover?

#1614 BUSINESS OR PLEASURE?—Julie Hogan
Daisy Kincaid quit her job when she realized that her boss, Alex Mackenzie,
would never reciprocate her feelings. But when the sexy CEO pleaded for
her to return and granted her a promotion to tempt her back, would the
new, unexpectedly close business-trip quarters finally turn their business
relationship into the pleasure she desired?

SDCNM0904